I0663683

Copyright © 2014, Revised 2021 by Jannette Quackenbush

ISBN-13: 978-1-940087-09-2

Table of Contents

Adams County

Ashtabula County

Belmont County

Brown County

Clermont County

Coshocton County

Crawford County

Defiance County

Erie County

Fairfield County

Fayette County

Fulton & Williams County

Greene County

Guernsey County

Hamilton County

Adams County

Cherry Fork Cemetery
14348 OH-136
Winchester, Ohio 45697
38.87959, -83.61529

A Grave Yawns

"Old Rhine Home, Graces Run Photo—" Now demolished.
Photo: Steven L Rhine—

On Tuesday, December 19th of 1893, 80-year-old Luther "Pitt" Rhine and his 71-year-old wife, Martha, were found with their skulls crushed and their throats slashed from ear to ear in their little farmhouse along a stream called Elk Fork, not far from West Union. They had been sleeping when attacked.

Sixteen-year-old Roscoe Parker, a boy of dubious character, who did odd jobs for the couple, had helped Luther drive a calf to nearby Winchester for butchering the day before. When questioned, law enforcement found Roscoe's bloodied clothing and a pair of Luther's stockings hidden in his bed along with five dollars of the Rhine's money identified as being paid for the calf. The boy was arrested but never made it to court. Instead, an angry mob whisked Roscoe off in his underclothes, hanged him, and riddled his body with bullets.

Cherry Fork Cemetery where balls of light flitting from an unmarked grave have frightened people for years.

They buried Roscoe Parker's body in the pauper's corner of Cherry Fork Cemetery. On a hot August day in 1896, Maurice Hudson, a local farmer, noticed a strange sound passing Cherry Fork Cemetery. When he peered cautiously into the graveyard and to Roscoe Parker's grave, a ghostly man stood with arms outstretched and his hands spread wide. A stream of blood spurted from the neck, and atop the gushing blood was a head bouncing and bobbing. For many years, people claimed to see balls of light flitting from grave to grave at Cherry Fork Cemetery near Winchester when they passed. And many refused to drive their carriages and cars along that route for fear of seeing a ghost.

Old Adams County Jail
116 W Mulberry Street
West Union, Ohio 45693
38.795947,-83.546306

A Mysterious Haunting in a Jail

In April of 1895, the county built a jail on the corner of Market and Cross streets in West Union. The front of the building housed the jailor and his family, and in the rear, there were two floors of jail cells. Sheriff Marion Dunlap, his wife, and children occupied the building during the early years when inmates began to see a white-robed figure floating just above the floor in the hallways and passing their cells at night. Door bolts would mysteriously unlatch themselves, and prisoners had escaped their enclosures several times, released by ghostly hands.

One evening, as Dunlap readied for bed, he heard a loud cry from the cell area. He hurriedly lit a lantern and made his way to the back of the building. The sheriff had confined William Woods and Charley Bradley in adjoining chambers. As Dunlap came to a halt before the cells, he saw the men were both shaken before one began to tell him that a white apparition had drifted down the long corridor, making a strange hissing sound. When it passed by Bradley's cell, the man let out a yell. It continued onward, pausing at Wood's cell long enough to reach out a skeletal arm and latch on to the man's hair, nearly pulling it from the roots before the ghostly form vanished!

The jail around 1908. Over the years, visitors to the old building have heard the ghostly sound of music, and lights occasionally turn on when nobody is around. Image: Columbus Public Library

Cave Hollow
Blacks Run Road
Lynx, Ohio 45650
38.737702, -83.446919

Haunted Hollow

Blacks Run Road near the hollow—

During the early years, Cave Hollow along Blacks Run Road was once a haven for thieves who robbed settlers traveling through the remote regions of southern Ohio. The many caves there provided shelter from those who would hunt them down for their misdeeds. Nowadays, the area is a protected preserve. Still, those driving Blacks Run Road occasionally witness ghosts lurking in the shadows along the graveled road before they vanish into the forest.

Mt Unger Cemetery
2553 Mt Unger Road
Blue Creek, Ohio 45616
38.7853517, -83.2843511

The Hanging Man

Those driving on this remote road have seen a ghost floating in the cemetery.

Many years ago, in the long-gone town of Mt Unger, a man murdered his wife. Not long after, he suicided by hanging himself on a tree not far from her grave at the local cemetery. For years after, those who drove past the graveyard saw the ghost of the man dangling from the tree limb. Then, after the tree died, there were those traveling along the road that saw him as a lone figure floating above the ground with his head twisted at an awkward angle.

Serpent Mound
State Memorial
3850 State Route 73
Peebles, Ohio 45660
39.024735,-83.430372

Serpent Mound

You can walk a trail at the mound.

An ancient mound, built by peoples of the Fort Ancient culture, shaped like a serpent with mouth agape and holding an egg winds its way through a remote area overlooking Brush Creek. Some who walk the trail feel a mysterious energy emanating from the earthen structure.

The Hidden Bones

Wickerham Inn around the 1890s- Photo Courtesy: Stephen Kelley Memorial Scholarship fund.

Outside Peebles, there is a private dwelling that was once a brick tavern and inn along Zane's Trace, a rugged frontier path blazed from ancient Indian trails. In its early years, a stagecoach driver stopped in for a night's rest and asked a worker at the tavern to awaken him before dawn.

Before sunrise, the worker knocked on the driver's door, and there was no answer. When the worker opened the door to peer into the dim room, there was a terrible sight to behold—a gruesome scene of blood spattering the walls and entrails slopped on the floor. There was a bloody outline of a body on the bed barring the shape of the head. Those within the inn searched the building and property but found no other traces of the stagecoach driver.

Wickerham Inn nowadays.

Years would pass, and those traveling past the inn would see the ghostly image of a headless man standing at the upstairs window and walking the grounds. Then in the early 1920s, the inn was renovated, and contractors working in the cellar discovered a skeleton buried beneath slabs of limestone floor. It was missing its head.

Winchester Cemetery
South Street
Winchester, Ohio 45697
38.938516,-83.647341

Crying Angel

Old-timers have passed down that there is a grave with an angel at this cemetery that cries. Nearby is a small circle of children's graves. If passersby get too close to the angel, the dead children call out taunts, shrieks, and cries to scare them away.

The crying angel—

Ashtabula County

Ashtabula Train Wreck
Harmon Hill Road
Ashtabula, Ohio 44004
Park: 41.875201,-80.782753
Site:41.878333,-80.789577

Horror Upon Horror

Horror Upon Horror newspapers flashed across their front pages in exclamation of the wreck. And then came the ghosts. The disaster as illustrated in Harper's Weekly—January 20th 1877.

On the wintry evening of December 29th, 1876, a snowstorm blasted through northern Ohio, leaving a thick, two feet of snow on the ground in the village of Ashtabula. Winds were gusting a chilly 40 miles per hour. The Pacific Express No. 5 of the Lake Shore and Michigan Southern Railway moved westward across the tracks toward the bridge. It was going a mere 15 miles per hour, heading toward the depot only 3/10 mile away.

There were approximately 159 crew and passengers on board, many traveling for the holidays. It was a diverse passenger list of men, women, and children, both young and old, families and businessmen—some onboard had families waiting for them in Ashtabula, others across the U.S. in California. William Clemens of Bellevue was returning home from selling hogs in Buffalo, New York. Eighteen-year -old Effie Neely and her boyfriend were returning from a trip to Niagara Falls. Philip Bliss, a professional songwriter (he wrote 100 hymns including Let *the Lower Lights Be Burning*), and his wife Lucy traveled to their home in Chicago. Harry Bennet was along for the ride, a salesman who sold newspapers and other trinkets to train riders.

The train had two locomotives and 11 cars—two baggage cars, two-day passenger coaches, two express cars, a smoking car, a drawing-room car, and three sleeper cars. It had departed New York the day before, heading east. Only a bridge over the Ashtabula River came between the passengers and their destinations. It would not seem such a feat for the train to safely traverse the 65-foot span of the bridge like so many trains before. But there was something not quite right with the bridge, something that had gone undetected even during inspections. Years earlier, a tiny crack in a small air hole had grown with the weight of trains going across the bridge, forcing a brittle fracture in the structure. The frigid temperatures and the heaviness of the train caused too much stress on the poorly built system. Just as the lead engine cleared the west bank, horror upon horror, the bridge collapsed, leaving the rest of the train to plunge into the river and bank below. It was a 70-foot fall into the frozen waters. When the train hit bottom, oil lamps and coal heating stoves in the railcars ignited, and the cars burst into flames.

William Clemens was hurt and later died from his injuries. Philip Bliss worked his way from the wreck to find his wife still pinned beneath the carriage. He stayed with Lucy in the burning wreckage, and they both died in flames. Harry Bennet would live. A rescuer pulled Effie Neely from the wreckage just as the cars went up in flames. Her boyfriend died trying to save others. Effie died in 1960 at the age of 101, the last survivor of the Ashtabula Disaster.

Of the 159 passengers and crew onboard the Pacific Express No. 5, 64 were injured, and 98 died. Forty-eight of those who died were unidentifiable—crushed by the train or burned alive by the flames. It was a horrifying moment in history for Ashtabula and the families who lost their loved ones. However, time would pass, and new laws for bridge design were made due to the disaster. Those traveling near the area of the wreck have witnessed strange, misty shadows emerge from the river where the train fell, along with shrill cries bubbling up from the water. They float momentarily toward the bank and then disappear.

The site of the disaster today where ghostly sounds are heard.

Chestnut Grove Cemetery
79 Grove Drive
Ashtabula, Ohio 44004
41.85587,-80.78194

Unrest in Peace

The monument for the unidentified and unrecognizable remains .

After the Ashtabula bridge collapse, 19 unrecognizable victims were buried in a mass grave within Chestnut Grove Cemetery with a memorial built above.

But they do not rest in peace. At times, visitors to the cemetery smell the pungent scent of burning, while others witness ghostly forms appear, then disappear.

Chestnut Grove Cemetery
79 Grove Drive
Ashtabula, Ohio 44004
41.85587, -80.78194

The Mysterious Death of Charles Collins

Charles Collins's mausoleum.

Charles Collins, the Railroad Chief Engineer, would have been in charge of the inspections and overseeing the development of the Ashtabula Bridge during the time of the train wreck, but another man constructed it. Reluctantly, when asked to review sagging to the structure, Collins found flaws and brought the errors to the builder's attention.

Workers fixed some of the issues, but not all. Eleven years later, and in December of 1876, the bridge collapsed. Collins died not long after in January of 1877 of a gunshot wound and was buried in a large mausoleum in Chestnut Grove Cemetery. Strangely, there has been a longstanding question of the cause of death. Newspapers wrongly suggested in their reports that the bridge tragedy was a fault of Collins, then declared he was despondent over the tragedy and committed suicide. Others claim a vengeful family member of someone who died in the train wreck murdered him. Such, some say that Collins walks around the mausoleum in spectral form wishing he could have done more to save those on the train, while others believe he is waiting for justice served for whoever murdered him.

Edgewood Cemetery
4011 State Road
Ashtabula, Ohio 44004
Section 1 - Northwest area
41.870695,-80.773269

Family Poison

Edgewood Cemetery and the graves of the McAdams children.

In the mid-1800s, Alexander and Rebecca McAdams lived with their ten children on a farm about a mile and a half east of Ashtabula. Their eldest daughter, Jeanette, was considered beautiful with dark hair and a rosy complex. Yet, she had few suitors as her character was quite peculiar for her time. She would dress in men's clothing, sneak out in the middle of the night, and disappear for days at a time; attributes hardly fitting in finding a proper suitor.

One day, she found work in Cleveland and did not return for some time. Then, after a while and occasionally, Jeanette would return to visit her family. During the time of 1848 to 1851 and on separate visits, five of her younger siblings began to die one by one, each buried in a small family plot at Edgewood Cemetery.

First was 13-year-old Julia, who was preparing to board at an Ashtabula family's home to attend school. Then, on a cold evening, February 27, 1848, the family noticed a certain paleness to Julia's usually pink cheeks. She was dead by the next morning.

Eight-year-old Arthur and 21-year-old Abigail would follow in January of 1850 while Jeanette was visiting for the holidays. They died within a few days of each other, both convulsing, complaining of belly aches—Arthur after eating an apple and drinking cider by the fireplace and Abigail after eating a piece of candy Jeanette had given her.

If anyone thought it peculiar that the children appeared to die only when their eldest sister was around, there was no mention that perhaps this sister might have been the cause. Not even when summer came, and with it a visit from Jeanette and 14-year-old Walter collapsed with what a neighbor described as 'a great agony.' It was not a month later when 12-year-old Luther suffered the same symptoms while working in the fields with a hired hand, convulsed, and died. Jeanette, again, had come for a short visit.

Finally, on February 1 of 1851, Jeanette returned home from Cleveland. Her mother, Rebecca, was ill with a cold, and the wayward daughter had returned to take care of her, helping her take medicines the doctor had allegedly prescribed, a white powdery substance. On February 2, 1851, Rebecca McAdams was dead. And the doctor stated that he had not prescribed any medication for Rebecca at all.

Jeanette did not return for some time, and her father later forbade her to enter the home. No one could account for her whereabouts after she left a final time. Then many years later, visitors to the cemetery began to see tiny shadows floating above each of the graves of the McAdams children. They would hover there before a taller dark form wisped from someplace unknown. It seemed to want to scoop the tinier shadows up, but they would flit and flitter away, followed by the taller of the lot, before they all disappeared. Most believed Jeanette had murdered her siblings and mother with poison but for what reason is unknown. After death, it was Jeanette's ghost coming to the cemetery still pursuing the children for eternity.

Where ghostly dead children run from a murderous sister—

Kingsville Railroad Tracks
Ohio 193 and Tracks
Ashtabula, Ohio 44004
41.907805, -80.691481

Swinging Lantern

In the late 1800s, Kingsville had a ghost that walked the railway tracks and swung a blue lantern back and forth hailing engineers. It stopped trains before disappearing into the woods. Those who saw the ghostly form believed its presence was directly related to the Ashtabula Bridge train disaster along the same path, and the spirit was trying to stop trains from continuing on the route.

Kingsville Library
6006 Academy Street
Kingsville, Ohio 44048
41.890793,-80.675701

Man in a Tophat

Kingsville Library—1911 on West Main.
Courtesy: Kingsville Public Library.

Occasionally, a ghostly man in a tophat wanders the Kingsville Library before fading away. Some believe his presence comes from Kingsville Academy, an early school built on the grounds.

Kingsville Library in more recent years—Courtesy: Gale Wheeler —

Belmont County

**Egypt Valley Wildlife Area—
Louiza Catherine Fox Murder
Site**
*Twp Hwy 546 B (Starkey Road)
Barnesville, Ohio 43713
40.104476,-81.174702*

The Stalking

The site of the Louiza Fox murder and where ghosts are seen at Egypt Valley Wildlife Area. Nearby Egypt was once a small town originally founded in 1826 around a popular gristmill along Stillwater Creek. The area around it was later strip-mined and took the name Egypt Valley Coal Field. After the state took over, it is now called Egypt Valley Wildlife Area.

On a bare hillside of old strip-mined land at Egypt Valley Wildlife Area, also known as Egypt Bottoms, a lone stone with an inscription sits. It marks the murder place of Louiza Fox. And some have seen her ghost silently pacing there. Here is her story—

Thirteen-year-old Louiza Fox was returning to her family farm near Sewellsville on a late afternoon in January 1869. The young girl was a live-in housemaid for the Hunter family, a local coal mine owner.

One of the miners in Hunter's employ, 22-year-old Thomas Carr, had been pursuing the little girl relentlessly since the previous autumn. He had, several times, accompanied her from work to home. John Fox, Louiza's father, questioned Carr with a wary eye, but the miner insisted he only walked with Louiza to watch over her because of her tender age. Louiza refused any idea of courting the older man again and again. Finally, however, it was brought to her father's attention by Louiza herself that Carr had asked her to marry him some weeks later. The child begged her father to refuse the peculiar, threatening, and unpleasant man; she had no interest in him.

When Carr confronted the father to ask her hand in marriage, John Fox kindly excused the askance, telling Carr that Louiza was too young. Perhaps in maybe two or three years if he proved himself worthy by keeping a job and purchased a bit of land AND if the young woman, who would be closer to marriageable age, was willing, he could ask for her hand again. But during the last weeks of January, knowing her brief time working at the Hunter family's home was coming to an end, Carr's menacing presence had increased. Although Louiza and her father both thwarted continued advances and gift-bestowing by Carr, his stalking had come to a head on that fateful day as he followed her from room to room, asking her to marry him.

Noting Carr's strange behavior, Louiza's employer tried to persuade the young girl to stay at the Hunter house for her safety until they could take her home by horseback. Louiza politely refused. Her home and other family members' homes were close by and just off what is now Starkey Road and near the Egypt Valley Wildlife Area. Besides, nobody in the tiny tight-knit community, not even Louiza, thought him dangerous. He was just another seasonal worker offering meager working and social skills.

Carr had already begun to believe the polite rebuttal offered by her father was just a formality in asking for her hand in marriage. In his irrational state, the odd miner thought that the well-mannered rebuffs from the sweet little girl were only to please her father, and she was simply hiding whatever love or lust she felt for him behind her modesty. It was, in fact, her 6-year-old brother, Willy, sent to escort her home when worried about her welfare returning from the Hunter home. Carr had demanded for the last time to speak with John Fox and had threatened the man to give his daughter's hand to him in marriage—or else. John refused him.

After Willy and Louiza began to walk home, Carr waylaid the two on the path. She tried desperately to allude him along the isolated roadway by running and hiding at some points. Then as Louiza and her little brother passed a small chestnut orchard a stone's throw from home, Carr made his move and crept from beside a fence by the trees and into their path. After sending the younger brother on his way, Carr asked the girl to marry him once again. She refused, telling him that she was far too young to be wed.

Carr then pulled a razor from his pocket, and tossed her by one shoulder to the ground. She called out in sobbing screams for her papa, and Thomas Carr slit her throat. By the time her father had hastened to the spot, he had found young Louiza lying dead in a small ditch by the road where Carr had dragged her during the short struggle.

There is a stone in Belmont County tucked into the Egypt Valley Wildlife Area marking the place where Carr murdered Louiza. It is not the only sign Carr killed her there—her ghost walks the grassy hillside. She is silent because the razor to her throat spoilt any ghostly screams for help.

Carr was hunted down, found guilty of murder, and eventually hanged. They buried him in an unmarked grave at the Methodist Cemetery in St Clairsville. Before death, he confessed to killing fourteen others, although some believed he fabricated most of those murders. But there was one confession many believed did hold some truth. Among those Carr acknowledged killing was another man—a German immigrant by the name of Alois Ulrich. Along with Joseph Eisele (also known as the Parkersburg Hatchet Slayer), he admitted to helping murder the man by bashing his head to a pulp with a stone in the Wheeling Tunnel in June of 1867 for the small amount of money in Ulrich's pocket. The body of Ulrich was dragged from the tunnel and concealed in a culvert.

Hempfield Tunnel in Wheeling just over the Ohio line where another ghost from Carr's murdering hand may haunt.

After death, Ulrich was not silent. Not long after the murder in Wheeling Tunnel, the ghostly form of the murdered man began to appear emerging on the ceiling swathed in the green slime, indeed gathered from the dead patrons left in an old cemetery above the tunnel along with his own rotten flesh. His arm extended with bloody fingers hanging half-severed from the stems.

The forefinger of the other hand pointed desperately at his temple where a gash lay, fresh but with dark, clotted blood. With unmoving lips, those who ran into the ghost of Ulrich would hear his blood-curdling moans and listen to the fight ensue that left him dead before the guttural words came from his throat: "Let the dead rest!"

You can visit the sites, and perhaps see at least two of the ghosts that one monster left behind. But be wary. Not far from the memorial for little Louiza, there was once a coal heap for the Fox's home. It is there that Thomas Carr would later creep up into the shadows before he was apprehended.

He hid behind the dump with a gun he had procured from a neighbor. The killer crouched there for hours, lurking, listening to the family mourn, waiting, watching, stalking the girl even after death. He returned there to collect Louiza and her soul to keep forever, like a ghoul returning to a grave to feast upon the remains.

His dark spirit is there even today. If you are not careful, he might not see the ghost of sweet Louiza who is said to pass by the grassy lawn and relive her horrid last moments struggling with Carr on the ground. Instead, it will be your soul the prowling Carr takes after he creeps up from hell. Then he will snatch you up and drag you back down with him and dine upon you —

The memorial for Louiza Fox at the murder site.

**Egypt Valley Wildlife Area—
Salem Cemetery
(Old Methodist Episcopal
Church Cemetery)
Salem Ridge Road
Barnesville, Ohio 43713
40.08920, -81.15360**

By the Grave

Louiza Fox Grave where she is seen crying at times—

Far back on Salem Ridge Road in the area called Egypt Valley, there was once a little place of worship named Salem Methodist Episcopal Church and, along with it, a tiny graveyard. In early years, a circuit-riding minister traveling to the sparsely populated areas would preach to the 18-20 members of the surrounding communities here before riding off to another remote site.

Now, only the cemetery remains, and there is an old tale attached to it that if a person walks around the perimeter six times, they will disappear. And local lore once prevailed that three witches were buried beneath a tree within. One of these witches brings solace to those a lover has spurned; if the rejected man or woman places an apple on her grave, she will reunite the couple. But, of course, it comes with a cost— she will take the rejected one's most cherished possession.

Louisa Catherine Fox was buried here after being murdered by the miner that was hopelessly infatuated with the girl. Passersby have seen the young girl standing near her grave, sobbing.

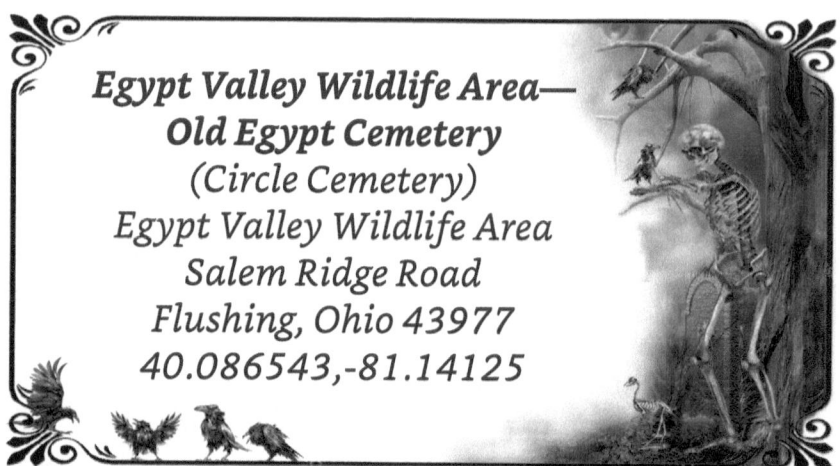

Egypt Valley Wildlife Area—
Old Egypt Cemetery
(Circle Cemetery)
Egypt Valley Wildlife Area
Salem Ridge Road
Flushing, Ohio 43977
40.086543,-81.14125

Fingernails Raking on Gravestones

Old Egypt Cemetery—

A little less than a mile past Salem Cemetery, there is another old burial ground that once belonged to the community of Egypt. It is called Old Egypt Cemetery or because the road circles the graveyard, Circle Cemetery. Even during the day, people passing by here have felt a sense of dread. It could be the wraithlike Black Dogs seen by bystanders, protecting the graves.

During the years of strip mining in the area, a truck driver's vehicle overturned here. When the truck rolled down the hill, the driver lost his hand and arm, and when they carted the dead man away, they could not find either. Some have seen the ghostly white hand working across the cemetery, its fingernails raking across the gravestones once in a while.

The road that circles Old Egypt Cemetery, and center, the cemetery—

Black Oak Road
Flushing, Ohio 43977
40.133052,-81.052544 to
40.111492,-81.022503

Walking Against the Wind

Black Oak Road—

During a winter in the 1800s, a young servant was sent to fetch the doctor in Morristown for her sick employer. She froze to death near the railroad tracks on Black Oak Road. She has been seen stumbling along the route alone with shoulders hunched as if walking against the wind.

Old Egypt North Road
67000 Egypt North Road
on to I-70
Bethesda, Ohio 43719
40.059327,-81.119883

The Legend of Lady Bend Hill

Lady Bend Hill—

Before it was called the National Road and before I-70 intersected this section of Route 40, the roadway was called Zane Trace. It was a path settlers followed through Ohio after traversing a hill with a dangerously sharp curve at the bottom. Many years ago, a young woman from Wheeling was riding her mare pell-mell down this section of road after a quarrel with her family over the love of a Guernsey County boy just across the state line.

It began to storm, and along this treacherous hill outside Morristown, one bolt of lightning lit up the sky and spooked the horse. The woman fell from her mount. Then, the mare dragged her to her death until her head caught on the trunk of a tree, beheading her. After that, this section of roadway was named Lady Bend Hill. Those traveling the highway have long been frightened by the ghostly apparition of a headless woman riding along the path. When a storm hovers above the hill, her high-pitched wails and the heavy beat of horse hooves echo through the valleys.

Buttermilk Road
Township Road 399
Buttermilk Road
Belmont, Ohio 43718
40.078416,-81.060532 to
40.084261,-81.124681

The Bobbing Lantern

A section of Buttermilk Road—

Travelers have seen a ghostly lantern light weaving and bobbing along the old road running beside Buttermilk Creek, where the town of Egypt once prospered. Most know that it belonged to a cemetery caretaker who froze to death one winter walking along the dirt path home and carrying his lantern to guide the way.

Brown County

John Rankin House
National Park Museum
6152 Rankin Hill Road
Ripley, Ohio 45167
38.750536,-83.843368

No Mere Series of Steps

The John Rankin House to freedom—

There is an old brick house sitting high atop a hill in Ripley overlooking the Ohio River. Along the steep and forested hillside leading up to the home, there are a series of wooden and stone steps. They would appear insignificant to most, except that the steps were used quite often during the darkest hours of the night and by strangers seeking refuge at the home.

They were slaves escaping from the south, and John Rankin, a Presbyterian minister, built the house at the site specifically so the steps could be used often by those who sought his help and freedom. Occasionally, sightseers walking the path up those stairs have been approached by someone from its past. As their feet follow the path of hundreds of escaped slaves, they hear the frantic patter of footsteps behind them. When they turn to see who is approaching, nobody is there.

The path many took in their daring escape from the south— and where ghosts return.

Old Lafferty Road
Ripley, Ohio 45167
38.766114, -83.766137
Lafferty Road and Chicken
Hollow:
38.774345,-83.773953

Calico Lady

Old Lafferty Road—

There are many names for a group of cats—a *dout*, a *clutter*, or a *glaring*. If they are wild or feral cats, they have been called, for a good reason, a *destruction*. But the name for a party of three or more cats that sticks out best in my mind is *clowder*, which comes from the 1700s Middle English term *clodder* meaning to coagulate or clot like, well, a "clotted mass."

There was once a clowder of cats along old Lafferty Road in Brown County. They belonged to an old woman in a huge and decaying old house along a dark and nearly forgotten road that ran beside a rocky, brush-stubbled creek. As everybody else in her family had long passed, she was alone barring these old strays, and she treated them as if they were her children. They followed her around as such, weaving in and out of her ankles as she strode around inside and outside the home performing daily tasks.

When neighbors passed by on the rutted dirt path in front of her house to get from here to there, the old woman would burst from the door with her shin-length cotton calico dress blowing in the breeze. She would scream and holler to slow down, so they did not hit one of her children. In her clasped fingers, she would always have a dinged-up tin bucket she used to keep scraps of food within to feed her many cats. It dangled there, and she banged it furiously with an old spoon to catch the attention of those inside the buggies and later, cars and trucks. Rumors always prevailed that she was missing two fingers of this very hand because when she fed her nearly feral cats, they would fight amongst themselves to get to the best piece. Often, in their eagerness, they would snap at her fingers holding a tender morsel of food. Occasionally, the bite would cut deep.

As she made her way along her overgrown yard in pursuit of those speeding past, around her swarmed her clowder of cats, a lumpy glob of *moggies*, which are mixed breed mutt cats. There were orange tabbies blended with Siamese and Persian or who-knows-what to make a calico mix of oranges and grays, browns and whites. She would scream curses at those passersby, her yowls joining with her cats' caterwauls to slow down their buggy or car as they just might hit one of her tabbies. She was known to jog behind the vehicle for quite a long time.

The old woman died one day. Most think she tripped over one of her cats. After a while, when neighbors noticed that she did not show up chasing cars, someone brave enough to do so went inside that ancient house and discovered her corpse, mostly bones because, well, she was not around to feed the cats, and they had nothing to eat but the old woman. When they had made a fine feast of her, and there was nothing left, the cats scattered into the forest or died along with her. There was not much remaining of the old lady and her kitties but a gooey mix of clotted dried blood and desiccated skin and the woman's old tin bucket still held tightly in her skeletal hand. And there were also lots and lots of orange and white mummified moggy cat carcasses. Eventually, the house fell to ruins.

The old house ruins—

After, there were rumors that the old woman's ghost frequently floated from the home's remains and out into the yard. At her feet, the ghostly cat meows blended with her wails before she vanished from sight. Stories into the 1970s recounted harrowing tales of thrill-seekers taking the rugged Lafferty Road off Chicken Hollow that ran alongside a creek called Lafferty Run to visit the ruins of the house.

When it was still a dirt road, that is, and not a muddy, grassy trail. It was a dare. The driver stopped the car. One of the passengers had to get out, close the door behind them, and walk a raggedy trail ridden with creeks and rocks and hills and what remained of old Lafferty Road. They had to find the house and call out for Calico Lady. *Calico Lady!* Even if she was not nearby, there were still cats hanging around. Cats were running, and cats were lounging on the porch, meowing. *Calico Lady!* Sometimes, no one came. Finally, braver ones walked to the entryway, knocked at the door, called her name again. *Calico Lady!* That was when she came, Calico Lady, the phantom of an old woman dressed in multicolored clothing and carrying a bucket in her three-fingered hand while the clowder of cats scattered with yowls. And she got mad, really mad, and chased the ghost hunters away. Ghost or reclusive old lady, it did not matter. She scared many over the years.

Now the house is long gone. An old stone foundation remains, riddled with rusty nails, broken bricks from a chimney, and cream-colored creek stones. It is along the nearly dead Lafferty Road, a trail only a little bigger than the width of holding the arms out to the side. It ends in a field. The road is impassible to vehicles, barely on foot. The bridges once running over Lafferty Run are crushed and buried beneath thick stone. Fence designating private property runs on both sides, warning trespassers to stay between the lines. But Calico Lady is still there, tucked in the dead arms of the building and the briar-ridden field. Some say she still paces around the old roadway along Lafferty Run, where the path stops right about Chicken Hollow. Back and forth, back and forth, Calico Lady trudges with a crowd of cats yowling at her feet, banging her pan. She yells with her ghostly fist in the air at those who drive slowly past and call out her name.

Higginsport School
Gaines and John Streets
Higginsport, Ohio 45131
38.791214,-83.968351

Whispers

Bystanders have heard ghostly children's whispers inside this abandoned old school building dating from 1880 in Higginsport.

Clermont County

Utopia
3833 Main Street (US-52)
Georgetown, Ohio 45121
Church: 38.776009,-84.056359
Marker: 38.77621,-84.056518

The Drowned

The little river town was among a few dozen experimental societies founded by Frenchman Charles Fourier in the 1830s and 1840s. He wanted to build a perfect utopian society based on the equal sharing of money and labor by those within the community, hence the name: Utopia. In return for a small house and land, families would pay $25.00 per year and work together as one and hopefully avoid the turmoil and depressed economy that had tainted their society in earlier years.

Fourier followers built private residences and a communal brick house, but the commune failed miserably. Within a couple of years, the community was abandoned and sold to John Wattles, the leader of a spiritualist group. Their philosophies blended traditional Christian beliefs along with communicating with the dead. The closeness to the Ohio River caught Wattles's eye—running water was also of spiritual significance to the religion.

The moving waters were so crucial that in 1847 and against warnings of a flood, members moved a two-story brick building right up to the bank of the Ohio River. Only partially finished, 32 people gathered for a party on the rainy eve of December 13th, 1847. As a dance pursued, the Ohio River flooded its banks, surrounding the building and causing the walls to collapse. Seventeen of the followers were drowned or swept into the frigid floodwaters and succumbed to hypothermia. John Wattles and his wife were among those present but escaped before the collapse. Those dead rise here in the Ohio River, and their ghosts waver where they drowned along the flooded shore. Some see them as mists, others as dancing lights and apparitions dripping on the banks.

Remnants of old Utopia still remain.

Lucy Run Cemetery Road and Lucy Run Cemetery
3755 Lucy Run Cemetery Road
Batavia, Ohio 45103
39.04280, -84.19250

Lucy Run

Lucy Run Cemetery (right) and Lucy Run, the creek, (left). A ghostly young woman relives her last moments and searches for her grave.

In the early 1800s, the Charles Robinson family built a homestead along a stream near Amelia in Clermont County. Over time, the family and close neighbors were buried at a small cemetery on Robinson's plot of land at the base of a small hill separated from the creek by a worn dirt road. Sometime throughout the years, a young woman living near the Robinsons named Lucy was going to be wed to a strapping young man popular in the community.

But only days before the marriage, he awakened the family with a hard knock upon Lucy's father's door at midnight and during a thunderstorm. The father and daughter rushed to answer the banging of fist to wood in their nightclothes. When the door burst open, and the father held a lantern aloft, the face of the young woman's fiancé was exposed in the pale light. He declared hastily he had found another to love. He would no longer marry her.

Quickly, he left while the heartbroken Lucy sobbed into her hands. Then, in a miserable fit of anger and without bothering to change into day attire, the spurned woman grabbed up her young horse and chased the man down the mud-slick road beside the flooded creek through the stormy night. Suddenly, a crack of thunder exploded into the night sky, and the horse bucked, frightened. The stunned girl was violently thrown into the surging waters. She drowned in the torrent bursting past the shoreline and disappeared into its depths. Since then, her ghostly form glides up from the creek named for her, Lucy Run. She limps across the road in her pale white nightgown from the place she perished to the cemetery bearing her name, Lucy Run Cemetery. She searches for a grave she will never find because the creek never gave up her lifeless body, and no headstone was placed there to mark her passing.

The graves of Charles Robinson and his wife, Asseneth, and some members of his family. A harrowing experience of Robinson's daughter, Mary, may have effected the story of a ghost named Lucy. Mary and her spirited horse were trapped by wolves while trying to deliver a message to a neighbor. Unable to mount the terrified horse, she tied him to a tree and used him as a shield for an entire night.

State Route 222/Bantam Road
Intersection
Bethel, Ohio 45106

Dead Man's Curve

Dead Man's Curve—

A faceless dead man trudges along State Route 125 between Bethel and Amelia. Some believe his presence comes from a deadly car crash in 1969 when an Impala and a Roadrunner hit head-on, and four teens died.

Stepstone Landing
Across from
Moscow, Ohio 45153
38.846693,-84.23216

Man-head Horse

The area where river crews saw a strange creature.

In the mid to late 1800s in the area of Stepping Stone Landing, a strange creature appeared to crews on steamboat packets traveling along the river during daylight hours—a horse with a human head, sometimes flourishing a dagger.

Old Bethel Cemetery
3297 Elklick Road
Bethel, Ohio 45106
39.007096,-84.138468

The Old Woman at the Gate

There is an old Methodist church with a stone foundation, white weatherboard walls, and a graveyard along the bounds of East Fork State Park. The building was unwillingly abandoned by its community when forced to leave by the U.S. Army Corps of Engineers to create East Fork State Park. Nevertheless, someone from its past remains. The spirit of an old woman appears near the chain-link gate, and many believe she protects the cemetery from trespassers who do not respect the rules.

Smyrna Cemetery
3446 Smyrna Road
Felicity, Ohio 45120
38.83670, -84.08060

Glowing Grave

Smyrna Cemetery—

Old-timers relate that Smyrna Cemetery was built on the same grounds as the grave of a Shawnee woman named Sweet Lips who was cursed and killed by her tribe for betraying them, then buried in an unmarked grave. Those passing have seen her roaming around the cemetery on foggy nights when the moon lights up the sky. She is searching for her people so she can make amends. There is a gravestone within the burial grounds that glows, leading many to believe it is the area where Sweet Lips is buried.

Miamiville -
Little Miami Scenic Trail
Ohio Bicycle Route 3
Loveland, Ohio 45140
Hike a one-way, one-mile route where a
train derailed and a ghost floats
39.214825, -84.307848
to 39.227132, -84.310134

The Strange Light Bobbing

A ghostly light floats near present Beech Road on a rail-trail—

Those who walk the Little Miami Scenic Trail near Miamiville occasionally see a strange, dim light bobbing and weaving along the old railroad tracks. Some follow this glow, much like the warm flame within a lantern, only to see it fade away just as it rounds a curve. The cause of the light is explained like this:

In July 1863, John Morgan led Confederate raiders into Ohio. While there, some of his troops came upon the Little Miami River Railroad and built a barricade of cross-ties wedged upright in a cattle guard at a section of the tracks called "the dangerous curve" between Miamiville and Branch Hill. In the early hours of the morning, the Morrow passenger accommodation Kilgour passed through with one baggage car and three passenger cars carrying 150 recruits from the Clinton County militia traveling from Columbus to Camp Dennison. They were less than three miles from their destination, and all were unarmed.

The raiders hid in a cornfield and fired at the train as it passed. Within the locomotive, both the engineer and the fireman were alarmed by the unexpected attack. The fireman aboard the train was named Cornelius Conway. His job was to help watch for signals, but most of all, anticipate how much fuel was needed to feed and stoke the firebox to keep the train running—speeding up or slowing down when needed on hills or in an emergency. At the sound of shots, Conway snatched up a lantern and peered outside, noting the shots were coming from Confederate troops. He knew there was an upcoming blind bend in the tracks and just the right amount of fuel needed adding so that the train could speed up but still negotiate the dangerous curve ahead. Just then, the train rounded the sharp bend and came upon the point where Morgan's men had removed the rails. The locomotive derailed and ran off the track, and the cars detached and went past it with the recruits tumbling out.

These recruits, with bumps and bruises, were captured and released after swearing an oath they would not fight the Confederacy. The engineer suffered a broken collarbone. But Cornelius Conway and his lantern were crushed beneath the train. Conway was buried, but his soul remains at the site of his death, floating along the tracks with his lantern in hand.

Coshocton County

Roscoe Village
Roscoe Village General Store
348 N. Whitewoman Street
Coshocton, Ohio 43812
40.278752,-81.876266

Crying Matilda Wade

Roscoe General Store—was once stores and apartments. Then and now, it has a ghost.

Roscoe was a port town along the Ohio and Erie Canal in the 1800s, a community thriving on the transport of wheat and wool. During this time, there was a druggist with a store and living quarters in a building in the town proper.

His wife was named Matilda, and on a September day in 1848, she was washing clothes in the back of the basement of the building. She had been gone for quite some time before another tenant in the building came to do some laundry and noted Matilda was not there. After a short investigation, the neighbor noted fresh puddles of blood upon the floor and a trail that led to an unused cistern.

With haste, the woman summoned Matilda's husband. When he came upon the bloody scene, he insisted on following the trail into the cistern. Several men lowered him down to the bottom. He discovered his dead wife's body with her head nearly severed from her neck.

The cistern where Matilda's body was dumped.

John Gearhart, a hired stable hand and building caretaker, was discovered with blood on his wood-cutting ax and clothing. He was arrested and found guilty of murder by insanity and died in prison of cholera only a few months later. If old traditions tell us that murdered ghosts are laid to rest after justice is served to their killer, Matilda Wade has broken that custom. Now the building is an old-fashioned general store with home decor, gifts, a deli, and natural foods like homemade fudge, jams, and jellies.

Once in a while, workers at the shop see bottles fall from the shelves. One afternoon, a computer monitor fell off the table. Customers have heard strange sounds on the third floor. Some have seen Matilda near the cistern behind the old building crying into her hands. The soft sound of her sobs echo down the alleyways and disappear into the wind.

Roscoe Village
Old Warehouse Restaurant
400 Whitewoman Street North
Coshocton, Ohio 43812
40.279657,-81.876644

Ghosts of the Old Mill Store

Old Warehouse Restaurant—

There was an old mill store along the canal where boats landed and unloaded their merchandise. The upper level offered dry goods like clothing and groceries for those taking the canal. For many years, those visiting the building reported seeing a woman and a boy roaming the different floors before they vanished from sight.

The Old Cletus P. Reese Farm
Private
Murder Ridge

Murder Ridge

Murder Ridge—

In 1954, Cletus Reese lived in a rundown farmhouse in the rural countryside about 16 miles from Coshocton. Reese had quite a reputation. Not only was he a huge beast of a man, but he was also often seen rambling along dark country roads near his home by passersby talking to himself with his old hound dog following at his heels. Those who knew him kept a wide distance between themselves and the man; he had been released from the Cambridge State Mental Hospital only three years earlier.

It was widely known in the community that he was slow in thinking but quick in temper. His strength was so great that he could hold a fairly large hog under each arm and wrestle down a calf without breaking a sweat. It was a volatile combination brewing inside the man and just waiting for the right sequence of events to explode.

And it did. That summer, Clyde Patton, a 28-year-old school teacher and father who also made ends meet by selling cars, stopped in at the farm to give Cletus Reese a demonstration drive of a Hudson he was selling off the car lot. Not long after, when Cletus Reese's sister saw the car in the driveway without the driver, she became suspicious and called the police. Local authorities discovered Patton's battered body in a shallow grave in a ditch near the furrowed fields of the farm. Reese had beaten him to death with an oak club.

After questioning Reese, police unearthed a second victim—Paul Tish, a 39-year-old from Mt Vernon who had escaped Cambridge State Mental Hospital on December 8, 1952. Reese had shot Tish with a .22-caliber pistol when the two disagreed. In a shallow grave, searchers also discovered 58-year-old Lester Melick, a local farmhand who disappeared November 28, 1953. Melick made the mistake of hitching a ride with Reese.

Cletus Reese was convicted of the crimes and was sent to Lima State Hospital in May of 1966 on the grounds of insanity. He later died. Those who knew about the farm and its bad reputation started calling that particular area Murder Ridge. And some passing along the roadway near the old farm have seen ghosts there; it has long been rumored to be haunted.

Colonel Henry Bouquet's Camp
SR 83 near County Road 24
Coshocton, Ohio 43812
40.301163,-81.87712

Bouquet's Ghostly Return

In the mid-1700s, Colonel Henry Bouquet was sent to defend British colonies at Fort Pitt at the confluence of the Monongahela and Allegheny rivers. During one march, local Indians agreed to return captive settlers if Bouquet would not destroy their villages. Bouquet agreed and kept his promise, and two hundred men, women, and children were returned to Bouquet's care along with enough food and clothing to make the journey back to Fort Pitt. He has been seen sitting on horseback in the hills where his troops camped during the negotiations, a spectral figure staring out into the horizon.

St John's Lutheran Church Cemetery
AKA: Stockum Cemetery
County Road 123A
Coshocton, Ohio 43812
40.210267,-81.779429

Mary Stockum's Grave(s)

St John's Lutheran Church Cemetery—

Teens have taken the journey to search for Mary Stockum's grave for more than 50 years in the dark. They come to look for the two graves of the ghost of the woman wandering around the Saint Johns Lutheran Church Cemetery, searching for her head. Local folklore says there was once a lady named Mary Stockum who lived nearby. She had nine children. One of them was mentally disabled, and one day, her husband decided to kill the child and so he did. He was caught, convicted, and hanged for his crime.

In revenge for the hanging, Mary began killing off her children one by one. After the fifth one died, she too was brought to justice and was killed for her crimes. Then she was buried within the confines of the cemetery next to her husband.

Before she died, though, she cursed the land and the people around the community and said the rest of her children would die along with her, then one by one those in the town would die too. Everyone thought the horror was over, that her curse was just the rant of a crazy woman. But the remaining children she had not murdered did not recover. One by one, they began to die. When the sixth child passed away and fearing the worst, the townspeople dug up Mary. They severed her head from her body and left it in a shallow grave outside the boundaries of the cemetery, praying that it would break what they were sure now was a witch's curse. Then they plopped one gravestone on the mound above her body and one over her head. Now, she returns around the old ruins of the graveyard in ghostly form stumbling between the two headstones desperately searching for her head so she can complete the curse.

Mary Stockum's grave (s).

You can find the legendary graves. It is a long, pothole-ridden, muddy drive, then a mucky walk through an AEP/ODNR public hunting area. There are cliffs and drop-offs, ruts, twists, and two turns to the road appearing to stop in the middle of nowhere. The mud churned up by ATV-running hunters on the archaic County Road 123 is seasonally ankle deep in some parts, knee-deep in others. But between, there is a small hillock with graves that time, vandals, and trees have knocked to the ground. Among them, you will find a couple of headstones—one with the name Anna Mary Stockum who was the wife of Christopher Stockum. The two owned a 315-acre farm around Bacon and the area the cemetery sits upon now. They had emigrated from Hessen, Germany, by ship in 1836, a grueling eighteen-week trip on the Brig Aurora, and they came without a penny in their pocket. The couple spent much of their lives pushing back the wilderness on their plot in Linton Township and building the land, which later was a valuable farm.

The 1860 census shows the Stockums had seven children living in the home—Mary-18, Adam-17, Elizabeth-15, John-13, Martin-12, Caroline-11, Jacob-9. By 1870, all the children still appeared to be living. An eighth child, Solomon-9, was also listed in the household in the census. Adam, the eldest son, had returned from the Civil War to help farm the land. Caroline was the eldest daughter, and she maintained the home. Only one person is missing – Anna Mary, the mother. She had passed August 29th, 1863. In late August of that year, there were several other known deaths from people in the tiny community buried at the church cemetery. Was it merely some sort of flu epidemic? Or is there more to the story lost in time?

There are two sides to the story—one that shows on paper the family of Mary Stockum was a typical family.

They lived. They died and their bodies were buried in a family plot on their land in Linton Township. They had neighbors by the name of Apple and Gosser, some of which are buried in the cemetery too. There is also a tale told by word of mouth, by story passed down from one to another. It is more exciting, more gruesome, and a tale of a crazy witch buried after killing her young. There are scores of eye-witnesses from hunters to adventure-seekers who have seen the filmy apparition of Mary, heard her screams, been terrified by the ghostly apparition walking the cemetery.

Mary Stockum's grave—

An article in the November 11th, 1967 Coshocton Tribune by Joanna Ross points out the legend was begun by the sight of two gravestones for Mary, hence one for the body and one for the head. A local caretaker verified it was true. However, his reason was a lot less horrifying and had a more prudent explanation. Yes, there were two gravestones for Mary. The original gravestone was replaced by a newer one. The old headstone was plopped up next to the fence for lack of a better place to put it. Now the question is: which of the two stories do you believe?

Will you pass the story off as local folklore, roll your eyes, and chuckle a little beneath your breath at those who, over the past century, believed the rumor? Or will you take the more adventurous position and trek into the woods like many before you, see if you can verify the ghost of Mary Stockum and listen for the screams? Because there really was a Mary Stockum, and she really did die and was buried there. Hundreds of people swear they have seen her ghost, heard her yowls. They will tell you that something is there deep in the woods at the old cemetery. If you do visit, the area is hazardous. It is along a former strip mine, and there are cliffs and drop-offs. The road is rutted and muddy. You may hear screams, many have. You may see a milky white form along the way as some have sworn to have seen. And there could, quite possibly, be something more dangerous lurking. There are always secrets buried beneath the dirt along with the dead in ghost towns long gone with no one still living to tell us the truth of what went on that hot August summer deep in the farmland and forests of Coshocton County.

(AEP/DNR public areas have rules and regulations. Many include day-use activities only. However, unless you are looking for vampires, you should have no problem searching for the unknown during daylight hours. Respect the dead and those who are still living who might have known them) Seasonally, you may need to park near the intersection of County Road 123 (on the right) and 123A (left)— (40.209008, -81.785404). Take 123A to the left, walking the .4 mile back to the cemetery along the old roadway. The road curves, but it is a straight walk to the graveyard, which is on the right (40.210353,-81.779499) and within sight of the roadway. Not a suggested walk at night! There are probably day-use only restrictions.

Crawford County

Dead Man's Hollow
1601 Ohio 19
Bucyrus, Ohio 44820
40.762406,-82.875649

True Story of Dead Man's Hollow

On September 28th, 1836, a man was murdered in this hollow. After, his ghost has been seen along the roadway.

In September of 1836, John Hammer and his brother-in-law, Daniel Bender, traveled by foot from Pennsylvania over the Allegany Mountains and to Wooster, Ohio. Daniel, the younger of the two, was only 25-years-old and was along for the grand adventure, to see a part of the world he had never seen before. He was unmarried and carried about $30.00 spending money in his coat pocket. His companion, John, was 45-years-old and married to Daniel's sister, Catherine. He had a bit more money in his hands, about $200.00, which he would use to purchase land.

They paused in Wooster long enough to stop at the bank, then set off to Galion, where they visited a grocery store. There, they met a pair of men who offered to journey with John and Daniel from Bucyrus onward for both company and protection, as they were going in the same direction.

As the four men worked their way across the swampy ground outside of Olentangy, the strangers began to spar who could carry the most massive walking stick. When they came upon a marshy section and a smaller creek that flowed into the larger Whetstone Creek, John and Daniel took two separate but parallel paths. Each was followed by one of the two men they had met in Galion. Then, the two newcomers attacked Daniel and his brother-in-law from behind. One drew his pistol and shot Daniel in the back of the head. John was struck with the huge stick by the second man.

John regained consciousness and was able to flag down help at a local sawmill. However, he did not speak English, and it was later before a stranger traveling the roadway found Daniel's lifeless body. John Hammer did recover and purchased land in Crawford County. But it is his brother-in-law whose memory has survived the longest—the place of his death given the nickname Dead Man's Hollow.

Daniel Bender's ghost walks where he died. Legend states a man was rushing his young daughter to a doctor in Bucyrus by carriage sometime later on the same route Daniel and his brother-in-law had traveled. A deathly pale stranger hailed him from the road, and the man impatiently pulled over. Upon looking at the little girl bundled in a blanket, the stranger introduced himself and said that the child would not live to the morning. Disconcerted, the father snapped his reins and took off down the road. However, when the little girl died that night, the father swore the man who had given the forewarning was none other than Daniel Bender.

Defiance County

Defiance County Children's Home Cemetery
Defiance, Ohio 43512
41.346149, -84.421203

Giggles

All that remains of the old Defiance Children's Home open through mid-October 1914—a cemetery and little spooks.

The Defiance County Children's Home was in operation from 1884 to 1914. It sat on 22 acres and could accommodate about 40 children. The buildings are gone, the cemetery nearly lost to time except for a few sparse graves. But the spirit of the young orphans who lived there are still around. Visitors relate hearing soft children's whispers and giggles erupting from deep in the earth above the graves. Where the sounds arise, tiny dancing lights flit about and then vanish.

Old Valentine Theatre
(Gathering Place)
602 Clinton Street
Defiance, Ohio, 43512
41.283934,-84.363867

Little Boy Ghost

When this building was a theatre, many years ago, a little boy ghost was often seen roaming the stairway near the basement.

Erie County

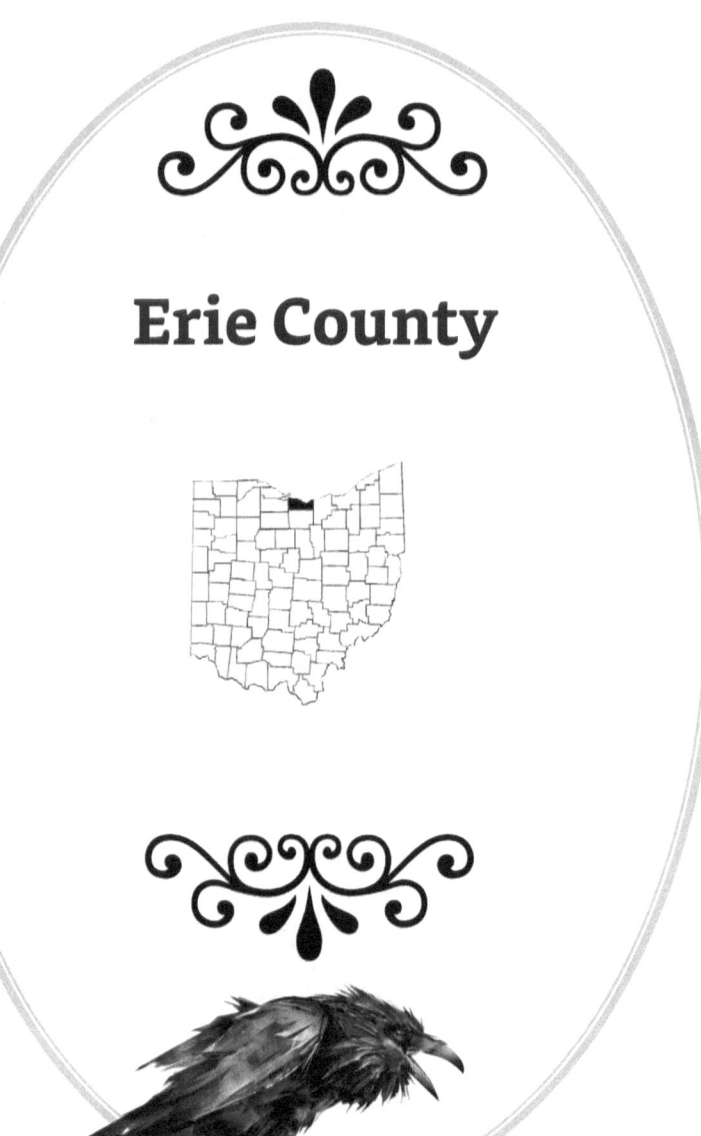

Milan Cemetery
74-98 Broad Street
Milan, Ohio 44846
41.29333,-82.598654
Grave: 41.293652,-82.596503

Knock-Knock on Abbots Tomb

Abbot's Tomb—knock if you dare!

Within the Milan Cemetery, an old mausoleum sits next to a dried-up pond. The tomb belongs to the family of Ben and Lorena Abbot. It has a legend tied with it. The mausoleum faces the opposite direction than the other graves, so townsfolk thought that the Abbots did not want to be bothered after death. Most left them alone. But, some people like to pester others and would dare their friends to knock on the door. When they did, the indignant ghosts of Ben and Lorena would yell at them and bang back. Although they have moved the bodies of Ben and Lorena, a couple of other family members remain inside.

Fairfield County

Stillhouse Hollow
Old Foglesong Road
(Now Stringtown Road)
Lancaster, Ohio 43130
39.765138,-82.596688
To
39.738016,-82.598523

The Half-Calf Shade of Stillhouse Hollow

Old Foglesong Road, now Stringtown Road—

In the early days, there was an old trail outside Lancaster that began above Coonpath Road and near a creek called Fetters Run. At first, the road was nothing more than a rock and dirt footpath from farm to farm and then to Lancaster. Then the root-ridden path expanded so a lone horse rider could easily travel its course, and later it was wide enough for a carriage.

Back then, though, it ran a rugged route alongside Fetters Run down through Christian Foglesong's property, Jacob Spangler's house, and a few farms owned by the Fetter family. It meandered past the rear of the Poor House Farm and to the Van Pearce's who lived closer to Lancaster. It came to an end where Rising Park is now.

Locals who traveled the route called it Foglesong Road for the family whose farm abutted a large portion of the road. They gave the small valley between the hills where it made its course a name too—Stillhouse Hollow for it was known to have whiskey stillhouses hidden in the glens and ravines. Many strange sounds came from this hollow.

During these early days, there was a ghosting on Foglesong Road. Those taking the road began hearing wails and screams coming from Stillhouse Hollow. It was a place few would venture after dusk, especially in the cooler days of autumn. One late night, Jacob Spangler, who lived along Foglesong Road, was taking an anxious horse ride along the rutted road to summon a doctor for a sick family member. He realized too late that in his haste to seek the doctor, he had taken the shortcut route along the section of Foglesong Road that ran through the haunted valley. He halted his horse and shivered past his fears. He had no choice but to go on and so he did.

He had begun to descend the forested hill leading into the hollow when his horse made a frightened snort, fixed her front legs hard in the soil, and began to quiver violently. Spangler leaned forward and squinted into the darkness, making out a yearling steer in his path with strangely glowing eyes and long hair. He tried to urge his horse forward, but the usually fearless mare refused to budge. Spangler, deciding that perhaps the horse's judgement was better than his own at the moment, started to turn her around.

Before the two could change direction, he felt something seize his leg. Upon looking down, he could see the steer was climbing up! Spangler was in such a shock, he could not move while the calf sat down behind him and placed his front hooves over his shoulders. There the two rode until the boundary of the hollow where the calf jumped off and disappeared into the woods.

Unnerved, Spangler continued to town and found a doctor to treat his family member. The two traveled the same route back to his farm. Partway, though, the same calf showed up on the side of the road in Stillhouse Hollow. It was the same place that a bloody trail had led years past.

A horse had come home without its rider, a man named Orndorff. Nothing was left but two empty saddlebags with blood and brains and hair stuck to it. A mob had followed the blood to the top of the hill and could see from the marks in the grass and soil where the man had fallen from his horse. They continued onward, following the path where it appeared the body was dragged from the road and into the hollow, continuing until they came to a house with a still nearby owned by an old man named Crowley. The doors were locked, but they broke through and resumed their pursuit of the bloody trail into a rear room. A foul odor of death and moldering sent some running out the door. When the rest threw open the door, before them lay a bloody corpse. But it was not a man, and instead, that of a dead yearling steer. The bodies of both the owner of the home and the dead rider of the horse were never found.

The Foglesongs and the Spanglers truly existed. There was at least one man named John Orndorff in Ohio, and one family was living in Licking County. Whether any fell to murdering hands, I could never prove. But the road was real (although it has changed its course and name a bit today), the creek is still there, and Stillhouse Hollow exists.

The ghost, too, was seen by many. Someone told me that the Fairfield County Infirmary was nearly parallel to Spangler's route with the calf-like creature on his horse. Was there an inmate/patient at the infirmary who might have scared folks for years by jumping on the back of horses? You can still see Foglesong Road today, and it is only a short drive from Lancaster along Stringtown Road. You can take your car along the road that follows Fetters Run near Coonpath Road, drive the same trail Jacob Spangler took on his horse that fateful night he rode into the path of the calf-like man about the area of Keller-Kirn Park.

A Stillhouse Hollow ravine just off Foglesong Road about 2 1/2 miles from Spangler's home.

Along Old Logan Road
Old Logan Road SE
Sugar Grove, Ohio 43155
39.617564, -82.553192

Dead Peddler's Tale

The road where a dead peddler would jump out at passing carriages—and later, more modern vehicles.

Old Logan Road in Sugar Grove between Lancaster and Logan has been known for 200 years as haunted. It was right around 1815 when the ghostly form appeared, scaring away carriage riders and farmers traveling this main road. Back then, Sugar Grove was little more than a few cabins dotting the hillsides and not the pretty village it is now. Pierre Bordeau, of French descent, made himself comfortable in a shabby, little place by the road. It was along the hillside not far from the location the Sharp family sells pumpkins around Halloween these days.

It would be Pierre's shack that a peddler would stop and ask for a night's sleep along his route. But over the next few days after, those who usually bought from the peddler noted he had not visited their homes. Many believed he had probably left Pierre's cabin during the night, so he did not have to pay for his lodging. No signs would call up an alarm of any foul crime save a small pool of blood found by a spring near the road.

Years would pass, and rumors always kept travelers away from Pierre's cabin. Nobody wanted to stay there for rest. The water in the spring tasted bad, and there were stories of a ghost haunting the road and hillside. It popped out at carriage riders taking the Logan Road route, the only rugged path that once ran a straight drive from Lancaster to Logan. It disappeared at the old spring.

Of course, no one suspected Pierre of murder. On the contrary, he was considered kind-hearted and had caused no one else any harm. Still, on his deathbed, he confessed to killing the peddler but refused to divulge the place where he had buried him. Local farmers searched for bones but found little save a decayed backpack with trinkets and the old peddler's clothing.

Then in the 1870s, the landowner hired men to dig a new well along the hillside. Upon excavation, workers discovered a decayed corpse beneath some fieldstones. Locals gave the man a proper burial, hoping that he would find peace. However, many years later, farmers coming through the area after dark still took a two-mile detour of that lonely spot on the Logan Road to avoid the ghost of the peddler.

Fayette County

Cherry Hill
OH-38 and Co Hwy 113
Yatesville, Ohio 43106
39.665178,-83.441091 to
39.682784,-83.415291

Headless Horseman of Cherry Hill

Where a headless horseman rides—

A headless horseman once stalked residents along State Route 38 near Yatesville. One pair of early tavernkeepers living on a small rise called Cherry Hill were notorious counterfeiters and ruffians. When a ghostly horseman began to show on the hill near their home, rumors wafted through the community that the innkeepers had murdered a federal agent secretly investigating their illegal activities. The husband killed the federal agent, cut off his head, and dumped his body in a well. They found his horse tied to a tree. When the wife discovered her husband had murdered the man, he tried to kill her too. She turned him into the police. Many years later, when a farmer was plowing, several skeletons were found on Cherry Hill where the inn once stood and the dead horseman rode.

Fulton &
Williams County

Goll Woods State Nature Preserve And Goll Cemetery
26000-26998 Township Hwy Ef
Stryker, Ohio 43557
41.556171, -84.367344

Calling Maryann

Most cemeteries are closed dusk to dawn. However, no worries—a little ghost girl wanders the woods night or day, so you may get a peek at her if you visit!

Goll Woods is 100 acres of land set aside from the 1837 settlement of Peter and Catherine Goll, French immigrants. A hundred acres of this land was left unspoiled and much like the Great Black Swamp area that once surrounded it. Goll Cemetery is within the bounds of the nature preserve of Goll Woods. If you stand in front of Maryann Goll's grave on a moonless night, you will awaken her spirit from its deathly slumber. A mist will rise, forming into Maryann before she travels slowly to nearby children's graves and weeps for their early deaths.

Greene County

John Bryan State Park—
3790 State Route 370
Yellow Springs, Ohio 45387
39.791886,-83.867748

Wiley

Many years ago, an old man named Wiley lived near the area where John Bryan State Park is today. He regularly traveled a much-used trail along the banks of the Little Miami River to Yellow Springs to peddle produce from the back of his wagon he had collected from his vegetable garden. It was customary that Wiley came once a week without disruption for as long as anyone could remember. He was a familiar sight to those in the community—he always drove an old beat-up wagon with an ancient mare, and he always wore a blue button-up shirt, blue-jean coveralls, and a red bandana around his neck.

After one particular storm where the water rose quickly and the banks of the river were swollen, the old peddler did not show up as was his custom. A few days later, the curious found out the reason for his absence. While making his way to town, both the man and the horse leading his wagon were pulled into the swollen river and drowned. Not long after he died, those following the path the old man traveled would see him strolling along wearing his signature clothing—a blue button-up shirt, blue-jean coveralls, and a red bandana. Then he would vanish at Meredith Road (John Bryan Park Road/OH-370).

Clifton Gorge State Nature Preserve—
2331 State Route 343
Yellow Springs, Ohio 45387
39.799667,-83.834574

Rosalie

Rosalie was an early settler in Gallipolis during the 1700s. At some point, she was kidnapped by Shawnee. A search party led by her husband trailed her captors to the area of Clifton Gorge. The two parties began to battle, and one Indian, in a fit of rage, murdered Rosalie with an ax. Her husband tackled the Indian who killed her at the edge of the cliff, and both tumbled off the overhang and died.

Rosalie's husband was never found; his body was taken away by the river. The remaining party of would-be rescuers buried the young woman where she lay. Since that time, those taking the paths around the gorge have seen Rosalie and her husband walking through the woods before they vanish into a mist.

Clifton Gorge State Nature Preserve—
Yellow Springs, Ohio 45387
Parking off Jackson Street:
39.794942, -83.828476
Walk Gorge Trail less than a mile to
Blue Hole: 39.795109, -83.839102

Spirit of Blue Hole

Blue Hole at Clifton Gorge is about a mile walk (1-way) with steps from the parking lot along the Gorge Trail and beside the Little Miami River. You will see it as a deep pool not long after Steamboat Rock.

Long ago, there was an Indian woman whose tribe lived near the location of Clifton Gorge State Nature Preserve today. She was in love with a man from her tribe. However, he loved another. One afternoon as many young men and women gathered for an outing along the pretty valley where the Little Miami waters flow blue and deep, she watched as a rival flirted playfully with her love. The man she loved, he flirted in return.

In a fit of jealousy, the young woman decided to force the man to choose her over the rival. She would hurl herself from the wall to the waters below. He would certainly see her falling, turn his back on the flirting woman, and rush to save her.

Thus, she clambered up to the highest rock, screamed into the air to catch his attention, then jumped. Instead of running to save her, the man turned to the young woman he had been chatting with and let his young admirer drown. Now, there are times when the evening turns its back to the day sky, and when the moon lights up the valley, you can see the young woman standing atop the rock. Her ghostly screams fill the air before she disappears into the blue waters below.

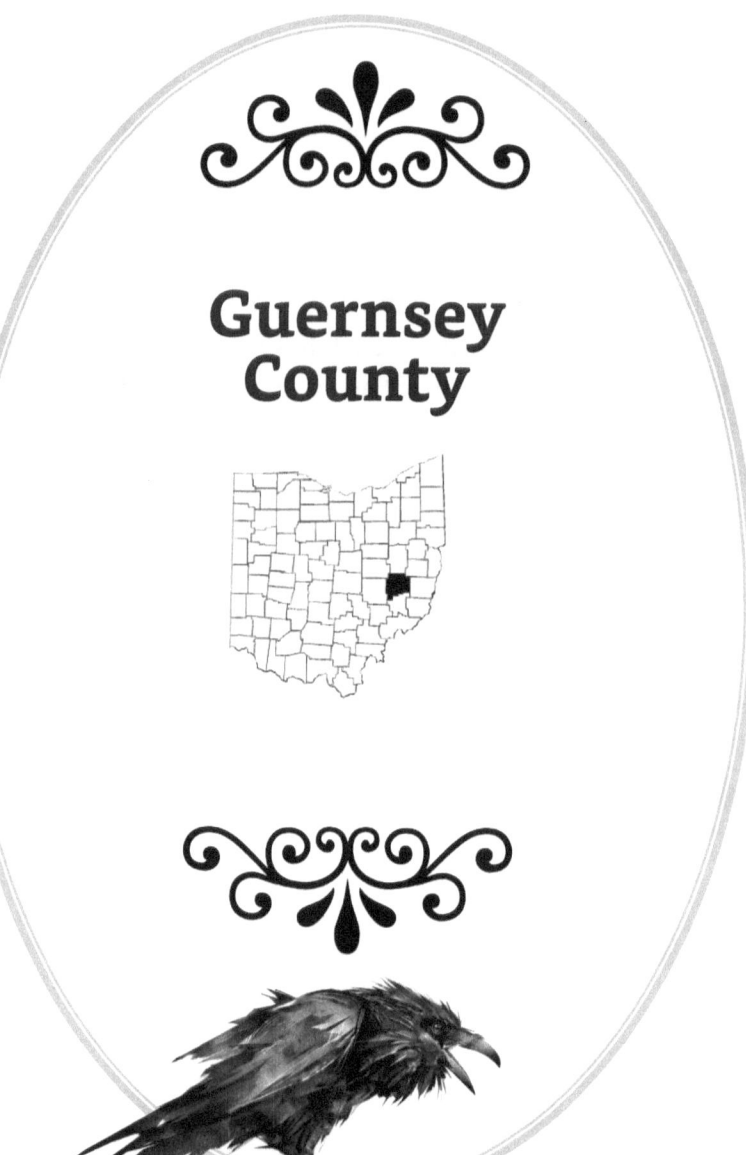

Guernsey County

Near the Old Tidrick Farm
Londonderry
22001-22299 U.S. 22
Freeport, Ohio 43973
40.14834,-81.315744

Headless Ghost of Londonderry

Where a headless ghost appeared—

Occasionally, those driving by have seen a ghost wandering between the woodland and Cadiz Road near Londonderry at the old William Tidrick farm. It has no head. If you ask an old-timer, they are sure to know how the ghost came to be, although they may not be willing to tell you.

One early morning long ago, a stray horse was found alone and grazing at this point. Of course, at the time, it was a fairly busy road by early Ohio standards. It was common for farmers from surrounding states to take their crops and livestock by flatboat along the rivers down through Kentucky, Tennessee, Alabama, and Louisiana. Then, they would either walk home or purchase a horse for their return trip through Kentucky's Wilderness Road and Ohio's Zane Trace. After, they could take Old Carpenter's Trail, now US 22.

But this case was both peculiar and different. The grass was trampled like there had been a fight, and the horse still wore its bridle and saddle. However, someone had cut the leather saddlebags, and whatever coins or possessions that had been carefully stuffed within were gone. Nobody claimed the horse and not long after it was found, the misty ghost began to appear to travelers as they passed.

Deep Cut

Deep Cut on the Old National Road where a ghost stumbles around looking for his head.

In the early 1800s, the government built a road from the center of the United States westward, which could become a primary path for settlers. Called the National Road, it would later be known as Route 40. One employee working in the early years on the National Road frugally saved every cent he could and stashed it in his pockets. It was noted by several unscrupulous coworkers who followed him one night along the new road.

They murdered him in cold blood for his money, cutting off his head so no one would recognize the man. They shoveled the small stones used to cover the road over his body near a deep cut in a hill they had recently completed. The killers buried his head elsewhere. Since the death, the murdered man can be seen in supernatural form, headless and stumbling along Route 40 between Old Washington and Cambridge at what locals call The Deep Cut, searching for his head.

Quaker City Bridge on 513
265-299 Batesville Road
Quaker City, Ohio 43773
39.968799,-81.300031

Ghostly Carriage

The haunted bridge—

It has long been known that a ghostly carriage follows foot travelers along Pike Street/Batesville Road in Quaker City, although no one can pinpoint the precise reason for its existence. If a traveler stops on the bridge, they will get a tap on the shoulder. Once on the other side, the carriage disappears.

Hamilton County

Spring Grove Cemetery—
Charles Breuer Grave
Section 100
4521 Spring Grove Avenue
Cincinnati, Ohio 45232
39.175175,-84.525829

Follow the main street entrance, which is the road with
the lines, past two shelter houses. Right after the
second shelter house, the road makes a Y where Mister
Breuer's monument is located.

Through the Eyes of Charles Breuer

Although Charles C. Breuer should have been remembered as a successful Cincinnati real estate magnate, his exploits before death left him with a legacy of eccentricity. Fearing his burial would not be properly performed when he died, he installed a mortuary chapel in his Clifton mansion with ornate mahogany coffins for his wife and himself. Upon death, he had a bronze bust built mounted on his marker at Spring Grove Cemetery with glass eyes matching his own. Visitors to the cemetery have long reported the eyes follow them as they walk past.

Spring Grove Cemetery—
Dexter Chapel Mausoleum
Section 20
4521 Spring Grove Avenue
Cincinnati, Ohio
39.168314,-84.526014
Go down the main street, turn left
at the first shelter house.

Guardians of Death

The Dexter Chapel Mausoleum is a private family vault built in 1869. It became the final resting place for 20 of the heirs of Edmund Dexter, a Cincinnati liquor distributor. Inside are 12 marble catacombs. A legend has grown from its existence that two ghostly white dogs will run past you if you sit on the steps. They may stop and stare into your eyes or even growl.

Cincinnati's Eden Park
The Gazebo
1501-1557 Eden Park Drive
Cincinnati, Ohio 45202
39.114194,-84.493479

Murder at the Gazebo

The gazebo where a ghost is seen—

George Remus was a criminal defense lawyer and bootlegger, becoming rich by monopolizing Cincinnati whiskey distillery operations. He divorced his first wife to marry his secretary, Imogene. While Remus was in jail for bootlegging, Imogene had an affair with an inmate pal of Remus, an undercover prohibition agent. She later divorced Remus.

In October of 1927, while taking a cab through Eden Park to get the divorce finalized, George Remus had his driver chase her down in his car, and he shot her in front of the Spring House Gazebo. He was acquitted of murder by means of insanity with a six-month sentence. Imogene's ghost has been seen outside the Spring House Gazebo crying.

Cincinnati Music Hall
1241 Elm Street
Cincinnati, Ohio 45202
39.109576,-84.519734

Back from the Grave

Music Hall—

People who visit Music Hall, home of the Cincinnati Opera and Cincinnati Symphony Orchestra, have occasionally witnessed ghostly figures appear and disappear. Their presence is easily explained like this: In the late 1870s, the city built a red-brick convention center along the Miami Canal, where once an orphan asylum, hospital, pest house, and potters field stood.

It later became Music Hall. During the initial construction, crowds gathered as workers turned the dirt over and dug up the rotting corpses of the dead buried there. Then, people began collecting souvenirs of the bones and effects lying within, some medical students even returning after police dispersed the pilfering lot to collect skulls for their classroom. Some suppose these dead have come back from the grave, perhaps confused or maybe angry and looking to put their bones back together.

Cincinnati Museum Center
1301 Western Avenue
Cincinnati, Ohio 45203
39.11018,-84.53616

Shadows of its Past

Before World War II, a train station called Union Terminal was built in Cincinnati that became a major center for railroad traffic during the war. Beneath its great roof, families would bid farewell to their loved ones entering the military service and leaving for war. Now it is a museum and mysterious figures pop up once in a while from those bygone days; shadows and voices linger in the air then fade away.

The Taft Museum of Art
316 Pike Street
Cincinnati, Ohio 45202
39.101875,-84.503136

Overseers

The Taft Museum of Art—

The museum was once the residence of Anna and Charles Phelps Taft, who later donated the home and extensive collection of art to the people of Cincinnati. Their ghosts haunt the building, watching over the collection once belonging to them.

Henry County

Olive Branch Cemetery
County Road 5a
McClure, Ohio 43534
41.383378,-83.971266

Carrie's Grave

Carrie Van Valkenburg's gravesite—

Legends have long prevailed that a young woman, bullied by her peers, is seen weeping by her grave in Olive Branch Cemetery. It appears that the torment to her poor soul continued after death as her marker was so desecrated by vandals searching for her ghost over the years, it had to be removed.

North Turkeyfoot Wildlife Area
US-24
McClure, Ohio 43534
41.413683, -83.989495

Lost Gold of Shunk

Near Shunk and in North Turkey Foot Wildlife Area.

In August of 1794, Revolutionary War General Mad Anthony Wayne had already traversed the land from Cincinnati to Toledo. His troops built a wall of forts along the way with his main goals to protect the settlers from Indian attacks and forcibly push Indians out of Ohio. He came face to face with Shawnee, Delaware, Wyandot, and Miami along the Maumee River, where a barrier of fallen timbers had been left behind from a storm.

The battle did not go so well for the Indians. Mad Anthony had three times as many fighters, and the Indians were defeated in a short amount of time and retreated. But in their grasp, they had managed to steal the soldiers' pay in gold sheets. Quickly, they hid the money along a bend in a river now known as Turkeyfoot Creek near the town of Shunk. They planned on returning later to retrieve it. However, they never got the chance.

The Precht Bridge before being torn down. The area of the ghostly rider can be seen at Turkeyfoot Wildlife Area. (41.413796, -83.989560)

The legends tell the Indians left the ghost of a dead warrior on the bank of the Turkeyfoot Creek to protect it so no one but those who hid it would ever uncover its secret place. Those who have searched it out have come face to face with the ghost who guards it—a warrior perched high atop a white horse. Long ago, a group of travelers came upon the spirit while crossing the Precht Bridge on horseback. It forced them to turn and go in the opposite direction. Many have dared to challenge the curse; all have failed. There is a price that must be paid for those who come into contact with the ghost, including a young boy in the 1800s. All have fallen victim to shock and loss of memory.

The Precht Bridge, now gone, was named for William Precht, who died there in a tractor accident. Occasionally, witnesses hiking the trails at North Turkeyfoot Wildlife Area report seeing his ghost coming up the bank of the creek.

North Turkeyfoot Creek and the old bridge before it was demolished.

Hocking County

Collison Cemetery
Near Hocking Hills KOA
29150 Pattor Road
Logan, Ohio 43138
39.468286,-82.489368

A Haunting at Blackjack

Aryanne's grave at Blackjack Cemetery.

Years ago, there was a town called Blackjack where the Hocking Hills KOA campground stands today between Logan and Old Man's Cave. Only a few homes remain along with an aged cemetery, settled on a hillside once John Collison's property. A ghostly girl walks from the area where the old homestead once stood, now the camp office. She makes her way through the campground, along a little dirt path, and into the cemetery. There, she vanishes.

Most believe that the restless ghost is a 16-year-old local farmer's daughter Aryanne Hutton buried there in 1893, for it is near her grave that the figure pauses. People have heard her whisper, "Come—" and "I am leaving—" as if she wishes those who hear her words will follow.

Exploring the ghost story at Aryanne's grave at Blackjack Cemetery. Above, Lori Hostetter, co-owner of Hocking Hills KOA investigates with campers.

Simcoe Creek/Valley
Off Tick Ridge Road and
Along Old Sudlow-Lee Road
39.424735, -82.370202
Pull-off along Tick Ridge:
39.424530, -82.380275
Trail is old Sudlow-Lee Road, rugged and a 2-mile round-trip. This is mostly Wayne National, but there is marked private property along the trail.

The Ghost of Simcoe Valley

In the mid-1800s, there was a young girl named Lucille Simpson who lived on a large plantation in Virginia. Her only brother died at a young age, so her parents indulged her with nearly anything she wanted. Few children lived in the vicinity of her home, so she played almost every day with the overseer's son, Robert, who lived in a tidy cottage not far from the plantation owner's mansion. The position of overseer had been fulfilled for many years by Robert's father, as had it been by his grandfather when Lucille's grandfather had farmed the land. As the two grew older, this friendship bloomed, and the two became secret sweethearts.

Robert worked with his father during the day, managing the plantation and also ran errands for Lucille's father. Knowing his overseer's hard-working reputation and noting the son's competency, Lucille's father hired Robert as a clerk and bookkeeper in the Simpson Plantation. Robert did remarkably well, and all went smoothly until Lucille's mother began to suspect something, and upon trailing them one evening, caught them speaking sweetly together.

She brought it to her husband's attention, and the man questioned his daughter, who happily confessed the love she had for Robert and asked for her father's blessing to wed. Simpson was quite furious as he had great plans for her to marry someone of equal wealth and prominence. No child of his would marry a common hireling!

Immediately, Simpson fired both the father and the son from their household duties and barred them from his property. He prepared to send his daughter to live with relatives for a short time until things cooled between the couple. Yet, even as the Simpsons made plans to send Lucille away, she and Robert met secretly. While Lucille was out riding alone in the meadow, she was thrown from her horse one morning. It was the week of her departure to stay with an aunt, and for days she lay unconscious.

When Lucille finally awakened, it was nearly Thanksgiving, and in gratitude for his daughter's health, Simpson decided to throw a grand party. In his delight at having his daughter recover from her accident when she asked that her beloved childhood friend Robert attend, the father let his guard down and consented.

At the party, Lucille and Robert immediately found each other. Simpson was well aware of the couple chatting a little too closely, but over the week between his daughter's request to invite Robert and the night of the party, he had come up with a rather devious plan to rid his daughter of the young man once and for all. Or at least curtail the silly idea of a marriage between the two long enough he could find a more suitable match for his only child.

On that same night, he invited the couple into his office and told Robert that he would consent to a marriage on three conditions. They would postpone a wedding for exactly four years. The two could not see each other during the four years, and Robert must leave the plantation.

Simpson also required that Robert make enough money to generously support Lucille by the time he returned. The old man was able to appear sincere enough about the pact that young Robert thought he just needed to prove his worth to them. Regardless, the couple had no choice but to relinquish to Lucille's father's terms.

Robert packed his bags and set off searching for a job, and a means to make his fortune. During this time, southeastern Ohio had coal, iron, and railway boomtowns due to the wealth of mineral lands. Word spread far and wide of an Englishman who decided to invest his riches on American soil and bought a great amount of land in the area around Raccoon Creek. He built many houses along soon-to-be-busy streets for workers and named the little town after himself, Zaleski. The area was flourishing in iron and coal, and the Marietta & Cincinnati railway went right through Zaleski. Robert heard of the ability to make a lot of money there and worked his way to Ohio and this up-and-coming community with many budding enterprises. When he got to Zaleski, the furnace, coal, and mining company quickly snatched him up for the bookkeeping skills he had learned under Simpson's tutelage.

For almost three years, Robert worked successfully, and his salary was plentiful. But then, Zaleski died in England, and his investments in the company town were lost. Most businesses closed, and Robert lost his job. Undaunted, the young Virginian knew that he was close to the amount of money he needed to earn to prove himself a worthy husband for Lucille. If he scrimped, found himself a meager place to stay, and worked another job, he could make up the final amount of cash to wed his sweetheart and make his way back to his home. A man named Shank would provide that income. He was a collier, a maker of charcoal for fueling the iron furnace at Union Furnace 16 miles from Zaleski.

Shank was a seedy character and a known thief living in a remote area of an oak and hickory forest, which he cut to make the charcoal. Robert found work with him when it seemed scarce everywhere else after the closing of the Zaleski businesses. They lived in a dilapidated shack with another worker far outside town in a hollow with a stream, Simcoe Creek, running through it.

Union Furnace—

Making charcoal, the burned wood residue that fired the furnace, was hard and dirty work. It required cutting a large amount of timber and stacking a pile about 12 feet tall over a pit, leaving a small chimney in the center for ventilation. A worker would light the top of the chimney with burning coals from another fire. Once the pile was burning, it was covered with leaves and dirt. The woodpile would burn for about a week, leaving nothing but charcoal which was raked and allowed to cool before being loaded into wagons and taken to the furnace. But the thought of returning home to keep his pledge to his Lucille the following year kept Robert's mind occupied while he earned his meager pay.

Simcoe Valley and creek—

Robert would often pat the purse on his belt, which held the key to his future, smiling softly, feeling soothed with the notion he would soon be with Lucille. This habit was often observed by Shanks, who eyed the pocket hungrily.

When the time came close for the four years to end, Robert wrote to Lucille divulging that he would be home the next Thanksgiving to take her hand in marriage as he had earned enough money to seal the pact with her father. Lucille was ecstatic as she had remained true to her sweetheart, and she had begun to make arrangements to receive Robert at the plantation.

Then one dark, stormy night in mid-November, Shanks ordered Robert to go with him to tend to the midnight rounds checking to see if the charcoal pits were burning properly. Armed with shovels and lanterns, the two set off. However, only Shanks returned to the cabin. As this was not common, the other worker asked Shanks why Robert had not returned. Shanks had replied that one of the pits was not burning, so he had stayed to tend it.

Robert never returned, and Shanks disappeared not long after. Most in the community thought that Shanks had murdered the young man for what he had in his purse, then threw his body into the charcoal pit. And what became of poor Lucille? When Robert never returned, she wrote a letter to the manager of Union Furnace. He told her the awful news, yet she always believed her sweetheart was alive and would someday return. When the Civil War broke out, her father joined the southern troops. A Union soldier killed him with a bullet to the chest during a skirmish. A battle played out at the plantation, and cannons destroyed it. Having no place to go and still grieving for Robert, Lucille went to work in a hospital, fell sick, and died. Whether Lucille haunts some old, southern Civil War hospital grounds is not known. Nor do we know if her father returns to the plantation to grieve the choices he made.

Simcoe Valley and the creek. Simcoe Creek runs through Wayne National and private lands until it flows into Raccoon Creek in Starr.

However, I do know the ghostly apparition of Robert is around. Travelers passing the area of the old charcoal pits in Simcoe Valley have seen a mysterious form of a man ooze up from the earth, then slowly trudge to the place where the shack belonging to Shank once stood. Then it disappears.

Jackson County

Salem Church Cemetery
Route 124 and Salem Road
Wellston, Ohio 45692
39.078658, -82.501895

The Knock-knock Ghost

The Salem Cemetery is the site of the monument honoring the unknown Confederates killed during a Civil War battle nearby when General John Morgan made his infamous raid through Ohio in July of 1863. Several of Morgan's men were killed when they crossed paths with Ohio militia on the hillsides of nearby Berlin Crossroads. Between 4 and 12 were killed, have been buried nearby, and may haunt the cemetery. The church is home to the Knock-knock Ghost. If you knock-knock gently on the door, you may hear someone—or *something* knock-knock back.

Knox County

Tom McMahon's Old Farm
(now private property)
Dodd Road
Glenmont, Ohio 44628

A Ghost in Brinkhaven

The farm where the ghost walked—

Many years ago, an old man named Tom McMahon lived a solitary life in an aged farmhouse along the shoreline of the Mohican River about a mile and a half from Brinkhaven. He was known to keep quite a bit of cash around his home, and one autumn day in 1928, a thief broke into the house, murdered the man, and stole his money. Not long after townspeople discovered his corpse, people began to see his ghost. He would hover around his home and even walk out into the road before vanishing.

Marion County

Old City Hall and Fire Department
*Corner of S Prospect and
W Church Streets
Marion, Ohio 43302
40.587435,-83.13004*

Ghost of the One-legged Shoestring Peddler

City Hall in the early 1900s where one-legged, dead Shoestring Jack could be heard dragging his leg across the floor.

In 1909, prisoners confined at the Marion Jail often complained of seeing the ghost of a one-legged shoestring peddler, nicknamed 'Shoestring Jack,' who had committed suicide in Cell 1 only six months earlier. He had hung himself by tying a pair of his shoestrings about his neck and choked to death.

The sleeping quarters for the city firemen who were on duty were located just above the jail. Ira Shrock, a local fireman, reported that he was awakened at night more than once by the crunch and grind of the dead shoestring peddler's wooden leg dragging across the gritty cement floor. *Crunch. Drag. Crunch. Drag. Crunch.* Not far behind came the ghostly apparition of the shoestring peddler himself. Ira Shrock did not sleep well.

Where the city hall and fire department once stood is a parking lot. Perhaps the ghost still wanders there!

The Old City Hall and Fire Department building was on the corner of South Prospect and W Church Streets in Marion. It is not there anymore. Instead, a parking lot has taken its place. I wonder if folks parking there at night still hear the crunch and drag of that old peg leg of Shoestring Jack's working its way across the cement floor—*Crunch. Drag. Crunch. Drag. Crunch.* Or perhaps if you have parked there before, now that you know about the ghost of the one-legged shoestring peddler, you will not use the lot there anymore.

Marion Cemetery
620 Delaware Avenue
Marion, Ohio 43302
40.576673,-83.121992

Grave with the Glowing Eyes

The eyes of the Sweney grave in Marion Cemetery glow. Although they state it has a scientific explanation, Josh Simpkins and Seth Hunt, authors of Haunted Marion, Ohio, actually checked this out. When they let their flashlight shine on the eyes and turned it off, sure enough, the eyes shone a dull green.

Grave in the Road
9 Cardington Road
Marion, Ohio 43302
40.513734,-83.016093

A Grimm Grave by the Side of the Road

On October 6, 1833 John Grimm was killed by a falling tree. It was on Cardington Road and he was buried in the exact spot he died.

Hinamon Woods to Marion
Marion, Ohio 43302
40.677595, -83.099195 to
40.614995,-83.130984

Little Lights

The area where spirit lights were seen.

In the late summer of 1905, mysterious lights appeared around Marion. One large light and several smaller ones seemed to start about 7 1/2 miles north of the city in Hinamon Woods and work their way in a straight line southward past the Central Ohio Lime and Stone Company Plant and Norris and Christian Quarries. From there, they headed toward the area where Marion-Williamsport Road meets with the railroad. Finally, they moved on toward the Columbus Hocking Valley and Toledo Station. Many witnessed the lights, and some attributed the shine to the spirit of a brakeman killed on the Hocking Valley Railroad.

Medina County

Spencer Cemetery
99 Jefferson Street
Spencer, Ohio 44275
41.101086,-82.122112

By the Lantern Light

An old-time lantern wiggles its way through the cemetery, held by spirited hands.

According to local lore, some have seen an old-fashioned lantern passing through the cemetery. Upon closer inspection, it appears held by ghostly fingers as it dangles there attached to no hands at all. At times, a second, tinier light joins along. Some stories relate that you can walk right up to the lamplight and pass your hands through it.

Morrow County

Vails Cross Roads
Centerburg, Ohio 43011
40.365119,-82.753447
to
Bloomfield Cemetery
40.378901,-82.723449

The Strange Confession

A ghostly rider once roamed this road.

A ghost rides on horseback in Vail's Cross Roads along the area where West Liberty-Mt Vernon Road crosses OH-656. It travels about two miles along OH-656 until the highway forms a sharp veer to the right at Rich Hill Bloomfield Road. There it stops at the Bloomfield Cemetery and vanishes. The ghost's story goes like this:

During the late 1800s, there was a house at Vail's Cross Roads in Morrow County. It was tumbledown and vacant, a home many would reside in, but few would remain for long.

However, it was not always empty. Salo Bintern lived in the house in the 1850s, along with his wife and four sons. The father was frugal and kept to himself. He seemed honest but always gave an impression of having more money than his meager farm would appear to produce. He would appear and then disappear from home for days at a time. There were always suspicious rumors amongst his neighbors questioning his whereabouts, yet no one could pinpoint any mischief he might have caused.

One day a wealthy stock buyer came to town looking for a place to farm. He stopped for a few days at the Vail's Hotel owned by Benjamin and Mary Vail. It was not long before Salo Bintern popped into the inn, too, from his home nearby. He conversed with the traveler, suggesting he might show the man around the community and help him find an attractive piece of property. Old Bintern also invited the prospective land buyer to stay at his home so the two could leave at an early hour the next morning and not awaken the others staying at the inn. The stock buyer agreed and went home with Bintern that evening.

After that, no one ever saw the wealthy stock buyer again. He disappeared. This would be of little significance because people do come and go. There was only one problem—travelers along the route found his horse the following day minus the rider and the saddlebags. Bintern bought a brand new farm. Years would pass, and sometime later, people started seeing the ghost, although they could not identify to whom it belonged. That is, until one day, a strange old man appeared in the infirmary in Morrow County looking for a comfortable place to die. He refused to give his personal information at first, then finding out he must offer up some evidence that he was a resident to receive a room at the institution, the old man divulged his name was Bintern. He was a local in the county long ago.

It was easy to tell that he would not be there long when the dying man settled in. After staying there for about two weeks, he asked permission to meet privately with the infirmary superintendent, and of course, the administrators granted the request. When the superintendent arrived, Bintern told him that he had a transgression he must divulge, but he must have the superintendent's solemn word that it would not be shared until the old man was dead. The superintendent agreed and received a full confession pertaining to a stranger who had visited Vail's Cross Roads years ago.

After, the superintendent secretly went to the house and found within bits of saddlebags where the dying man stated they would be located. Bintern had beaten the stock buyer to death while he slept in the bed at his homestead. But if the killer divulged his misdeed, does that murdered traveler still ride the roadway to the cemetery and stop there? Some say he does.

Vail Cross Roads. Does a ghost still travel these roads? I have not seen him on my trips through—yet, that is.

Sandusky County

Big Island
Pipe Creek Wildlife Area
1st Street and River Avenue
Sandusky, Ohio 44870
41.44860,-82.67027

Mysterious Lights at Big Island

Area where the lights were seen, now the Big Island Water Treatment and the Pipe Creek Wildlife Area/Big Island Preserve.

In the early 1900s, residents of East Sandusky across from the land jutting out into Lake Erie called Big Island saw tiny lights bobbing across the waterway. Some believed they were the spirits of Commodore Oliver Hazard Perry's crew from the Battle of Lake Erie in September of 1813. The ghosts of the U.S. Navy men had returned to guard the loot rumored the soldiers had buried there before the battle in case the British Royal Navy captured them.

Sandusky State Theatre
107 Columbus Avenue
Sandusky, Ohio 44870
41.456815,-82.712311

Ghostly Relic of Vaudeville

Visitors to Sandusky Theatre have seen a ghostly woman wearing clothing of the 1920s. She is believed to be from the early vaudeville years.

Summit County

Stanford Road
Peninsula, Ohio 44264
41.277743, -81.549945

Hell Town

The Highway to Hell in its more modern heyday. Even before, this road was known for thieves—as the hill dropped, carriage drivers could not see robbers lurking in the woods. Those murdered for whatever cash they carried still remain as ghosts.

The area dubbed Hell Town has been known as the old ghost town harboring Krejci Dump's industrial waste, the region that a massive python roamed the countryside, and the place of a crybaby bridge and a satanic church. Now it is part of Cuyahoga National Park. But long ago, old-timers described it as the place where the sad ghosts of murdered early travelers robbed by highwaymen staggered along the roadway.

Summit Metro Parks—
Deep Lock Quarry Park
(Railway and Quarry Area)
5779 Riverview Road
Peninsula, Ohio 44264
41.230476,-81.554049

Spirits of the Quarry

Valley Railway where a headless ghost of a train conductor stands.

The old Valley Railway passes through Cuyahoga Valley National Park just as it did when it was built in the 1880s. It runs along the Cuyahoga River and crosses the water at Deep Lock Quarry Metro Park near the Ohio and Erie Canal Towpath Trail. The headless ghost of a train conductor has been seen standing by the bridge where it crosses the river.

Not far away and closer to Peninsula, a ghostly young man plods along the tracks.

Here, a quarry worker still heads home long after he died—

Within Deep Lock Quarry Park, Berea Sandstone was once extracted from Deep Rock Quarry to make millstones, canal locks, and local structures. It was a dangerous job, and falling rock and equipment killed many workers. Those hiking nearby often hear voices along the trail and nearby at Lock 28 of the Ohio and Erie Canal.

At the lock and quarry where phantom voices are heard—

Cuyahoga Valley
National Park —
Mater Dolorosa Cemetery
500 West Streetsboro Road
Peninsula, Ohio 44264
41.230992,-81.508301

A Ghost Walks the Cemetery

Michael Raleigh grave, and to the right of the cross, a face—

The Mater Dolorosa Cemetery is settled beside Cuyahoga Valley National Park's Happy Days Visitors Center. Established in the late 1860s as a private family plot for the Doud family, those buried within are mainly Irish Catholic settlers. Later, Mother of Sorrows Church held its deed. There are approximately 23 people buried here. One of them is Michael Raleigh, an early immigrant buried here in June of 1873. His face appears on his gravestone.

A ghost haunts the cemetery. When the Civil War ended, 21-year-old Thomas Coady was returning home from the Civil War in April of 1865 after a stint in the Confederate POW camp at Andersonville. The prison camps had been horrendous, packed full of sick and starving Union Soldiers who were now free at last. As were 1,700 other free soldiers, he was crammed into the overloaded Steamship Sultana, eager to be rid of the war and get home to his family.

While the ship was pushing along the flooded Mississippi River in April of 1865, the boilers exploded near Memphis, Tennessee. Thomas Coady was killed during the explosion, and his body was brought back to his family for burial in Mater Dolorosa Cemetery. Since he was buried, visitors to the cemetery have watched him walk the paths near his grave. Sometimes he startles passersby by peering out from behind headstones.

The cemetery where Coady walks—

Coady's grave marker—

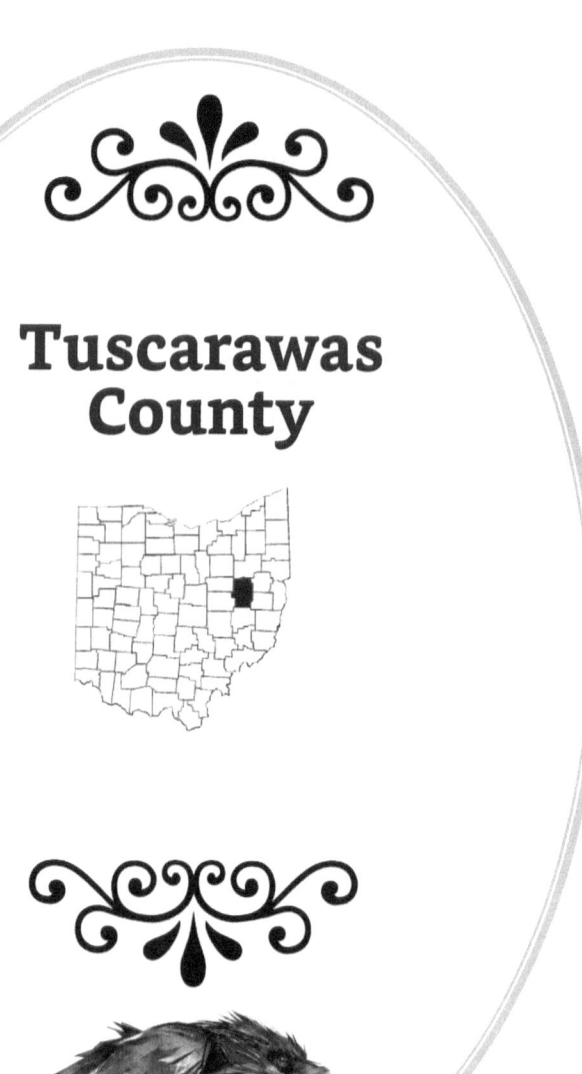

Tuscarawas County

Bridge Over Sugar Creek
1694 OH-39
Dover, Ohio 44622
40.512649, -81.488303

Ghost of Sugar Creek

The bridge over Sugar Creek where a ghostly girl would appear after her murder by a jealous wife.

In June of 1880, Canal Dover resident John Krause stared at something akin to a sack floating in the calm waters of Sugar Creek when he crossed the bridge along Shanesville Road heading toward his job at the coal mines. Curious, he drew off his boots and sloshed through the muddy water. Then he towed the object shoreward with a piece of rail until he saw what he thought was a striped coverlet sewn into a sack. Not wanting to open the bag, the man released it to the water's current and continued to work.

Krause mentioned his find to the other men, and it was not long before he and a few workers, including another miner, William Deiser, would travel back to Sugar Creek to investigate. There, the miners hauled the peculiar package to shore while curious bystanders watched. Those who stood by leaned forward inquisitively as fingers loosened the sack that was lazily tied together, then covered their noses with cupped hands as the stench of something decomposing filled their nostrils. Then the material unfolded to reveal walnut shells, a calico dress, ashes, a brick, and a partially dressed, badly beaten corpse. In the center, there was a darkened, rotting-skinned skull stuffed indiscriminately against some clothing.

Authorities quickly identified the remains as 18-year-old Mary Seneff. She had been missing for over two weeks, and her sister, Sarah Resler, had visited recently and voiced her concerns to local authorities of the girl's absence. Mary had come to work as a domestic servant cleaning the family homes of David Crites and his son-in-law Henry Athey who lived in houses on the same property on Stonecreek. She also helped Henry's wife, Ellen, who had suffered a miscarriage that year and needed help with the home and children. Among their houses was a small community of close-knit families related in one way or the other by blood or marriage—the Fishers, the Crites, and the Atheys. Mary's mother and father settled in Indiana, but her family had once lived in the area, and her married sister, Sarah Resler, still resided in the nearby village of Barrs Mills.

However, early in June, Sarah had gotten a letter from Mary stating she had left to visit her mother in Indiana. Not only did a misspelling of Mary's last name tip Sarah off as being peculiar, but it was also unusual for the woman to go without notice to her sister beforehand—the two were quite close. The Atheys maintained Mary had left for another job .

Along with local authorities, the constable paid a visit to the Crites's farm on June 16th. A horrid odor oozed from the backyard. The men followed it to a five-foot ash heap and began to dig in the charred residue. Some cabbage stalks, calico soiled with blood, walnuts, bricks, and a rubber garter were within. Next, they went to a wagon in the barnyard and found it was wet and muddy and held coal ashes. There was an ax also in the carriage with blood on the head. Inside the home, they found shoe buttons in the stove and stationary with handwriting matching fraudulent letters sent to Mary's sister stating the young domestic servant had left for her mother's home.

Ellen Athey was arrested and jailed. She confessed she had committed the crime in a jealous rage, believing young Mary was making passes at her husband. She had a dream Mary was having an affair with her husband, and the jealousy slowly began to nibble away at her sanity. Ellen murdered poor Mary with an ax and buried her in the yard. But the stench of the body decomposing bade her ask her family to help her dispose of it farther away. The body was dug up, wrapped in material, and weighted down with bricks before tossing it into Sugar Creek. The arrest of her husband, Henry Athey, and brothers 24-year-old Alexander and 16-year-old Frank Crites came directly after for helping her dispose of the body. It would be several months before Alexander and Henry were released. Only Ellen went to trial.

Mary's ghost began to show up where the men tossed her body over the old iron bridge above the Sugar Creek. It was not just one, but many who saw a misty form in the water rise up and take the shape of a woman so clearly, she was recognizable. Mary's ghost would try to address some with arms open wide. Others, she passed, walking from the bridge and toward the home where the murder took place.

Ridge Road Cemetery
Aka Rehobeth Cemetery
Ridge Road NE & University Drive NE
New Philadelphia, Ohio 44663
40.479694,-81.379187

Warlock's Grave

The grave dubbed "Warlock's Grave—"

Local legends say a man accused of being a warlock is buried at Rehobeth Cemetery. His head was cut off and laid near his feet. Each year, the head moves slowly upward until it reaches his hands. Then, he will be able to place his head back on his shoulders and rise again. Actually, the grave belongs to Ransom Newton (1808—1875), the father of fourteen children. The land where the cemetery lies originally held a Methodist Church, Rehobeth Church, and the property it sat upon was donated by Ransom Newton. He died in 1875 at the age of 67.

**Centenary Cemetery
And Winding Staircase Road**
2201 Centenary Hill Road SW
Port Washington, Ohio 43837
40.2942,-81.518535

Haunted by Its Past

Forms have been seen rising from the graves at this old cemetery at night. People have experienced thunder, lightning, and heavy winds while driving along the road leading to it on cloudless days, all blamed on cult activity in the area years earlier.

Gnadenhutten Memorial
Gnadenhutten Historical Park
and Museum
352 S. Cherry Street
Gnadenhutten, Ohio 44629
40.355354,-81.435289

They Will Not Rest

A place of great unrest—

Those who visit Gnadenhutten Historical Park occasionally hear mysterious screams and voices. When the curious seek out the cause of the noise, they cannot locate the source. The reason for the sounds are explained like this—David Zeisberger founded the Moravian Church mission in Gnadenhutten in 1772 to convert local Native Indians to Christianity. Although the white settlers and the Indians lived peacefully, British-allied Delaware forced Christian Delaware and the missionaries to abandon their home in Gnadenhutten in 1781 and moved the Gnadenhutten Indians to a camp along the Sandusky River.

In February of 1782, some of the Gnadenhutten Indians, starving from lack of rations, were permitted to return to harvest their crops at the mission. However, Pennsylvania militia accused them of attacking settlers and murdered them. The noises are always near the buildings where the militia slaughtered nearly 90 of the Indians—men, women, and children. Now they will not rest.

Post Boy Road
5654-5786 Post Boy Road
Newcomerstown, Ohio 43832
Between: 40.227678,-81.582609
And 40.229562,-81.573735

Post Boy's Story

In September of 1825, 20-year-old William Cartmell, a government mail carrier, was delivering letters along the isolated roads of the county. His job necessitated taking the mail from Freeport to his hometown of Coshocton, a route of about 40 miles. He passed through the Cadiz and Coshocton Road along his path, often used by stock buyers and merchants selling their livestock.

On one certain day, a drover called Smeltzer was also making his way along the same route, heading homeward with a large amount of money after delivering livestock at a sale. An unscrupulous man named John Funston heard that Smeltzer would be coming along the road and planned to rob the drover of his cash. As he lay in wait for an ambush, William Cartmell rode into his view. Eyeing the heavily ladened satchels and believing the young post boy was the drover, Funston murdered and robbed Cartmell.

John Funston was caught and later executed—a ten-dollar bill given to Cartmell by the postmaster was recognized by its numbers when Funston used it to pay a gunsmith, and the gunsmith purchased dry goods at the store. For many years, travelers along the course Cartmell took as a post boy would see him riding past in ghostly form. He was even known to stop at places along his old route, startling those within before vanishing.

Stone Quarry
2942 Brightwood Road SE
New Philadelphia, Ohio 44663
40.431939,-81.376294

Three Lights

The cliff where the lights are witnessed—

In the late 1700s, a Mingo married an English woman, whom he left after many years when he fell in love with a Mingo woman. The Mingo couple's favorite place to visit was a cliff, and the English woman tracked them down there one night. Seeing the two together, she rushed forward in a rage to push them off but went over the edge along with the couple. Some have seen three lights at the top of the cliff before they flit downward, spiraling as the man and the two women did so long ago.

Schoenbrunn Village
1984 E. High Avenue
New Philadelphia, Ohio 44663
40.467078,-81.413008

The Village

Schoenbrunn Village was first settled in 1772 by Moravian missionaries whose commitment was to convert Native Indians to Christianity. It would prosper until 1777 with 60 dwellings and 300 Moravian missionaries and Delaware until the American Revolution when the village was moved closer to Coshocton for safety. It appears some of those living there never left, though. Visitors to the town have seen ghostly lights floating along with strange noises.

Zoar Village State Memorial
198 Main Street
Zoar, Ohio 44697

The Ghosts of Zoar Village

The village of Zoar was founded in 1817 by a group of German farmers who wanted to live apart from society in a communal group so they could practice their religious beliefs freely. By 1898, the group disbanded, but the town lives on. A few spirits have chosen to stick around, too—

Canal Tavern of Zoar
8806 Towpath Road NE.
Zoar, Ohio 44697
40.607974,-81.428694

Opened for guests in 1829 as a tavern and hotel for travelers, it still offers both food and drink to those venturing to Zoar. The spirit of a sick man who stayed there and died while traveling along the canal haunts the building. He was buried by town members, but his wife allegedly had him exhumed so she could dig through his pockets and find the money he had secreted there for his return trip. He is quite mischievous now, knocking things off shelves and stealing pots and pans.

**Zoar School Inn Bed
& Breakfast
160 E 3rd Street
Zoar, Ohio 44697
40.613504,-81.42219**

The building was Zoar's first school and was in operation from 1836 to 1868. After that, it became a residence and bed and breakfast stay. Small objects have moved, and the sound of furniture banging in the upstairs is often heard.

**Cobbler Shop Bed and
Breakfast and Antiques
121 East Second Street
Zoar, Ohio 44697
40.612991,-81.422385**

Once the cobbler shop where shoes were made for those living in the community, it was also used as housing for the cobbler's family. Now it is a bed and breakfast and antique shop. Visitors have heard knocking on walls and footsteps and have seen a ghostly figure of a man in a suit.

**Zoar Hotel
198 Main Street
Zoar , Ohio 44697
40.612594,-81.422358**

Several ghosts haunt the hotel built in 1833. Guests hear voices and loud ghostly parties going on in the hotel .

Vinton County

Moonville—Ghost Town
Hope-Moonville Road
Zaleski, Ohio 45698
Parking: 39.308325, -82.324495
Tunnel: 39.307389, -82.322434

Haunted Moonville

Moonville, the tunnel— Among the many small mining and railway ghost town communities along the abandoned Marietta and Cincinnati tracks in southern Ohio, one sticks out among the others nowadays for its reputation as being haunted. It is called Moonville. Although it was little more than a bit of land owned by the Fergusons and Coes, the tracks, trestles, and tunnel that ran through it were used by many to get from one town to the next as a flat shortcut avoiding the many hills in the surrounding area.

The number of trains and pedestrians sharing the track would make for many deaths—and more than a few ghosts.

An early ghost exploration in the tunnel where we had many strange and unnerving incidents, including this crystal circling rapidly.

Engineer:

A white figure has been seen carrying a lantern at the far end of the tunnel since the late 1800s when engineer Charles Lawhead was killed after two freight trains collided on the Cincinnati and Marietta railroad.

Baldie Keeton:

In the late summer of 1886, Baldie Keeton was found dead along the tracks after returning from court in Zaleski. A bully of a man, most assumed he was murdered. His ghost has been blamed for pelting hikers with rocks from the top of the tunnel.

Lavender Lady:

A ghostly scent of lavender wafts in the air near the far end of the tunnel. Many believe it is the ghost of Mary Shea who, in 1890, was struck and killed by a train while crossing the trestle that once stood just outside the tunnel.

Brakeman/Miner

A man walking the tracks home after getting drunk in Zaleski in the late 1800s was killed by a train after falling asleep on the tracks with a whiskey bottle in hand. Those who come close to the place he died have heard a man whisper, "That's mine" as if he believes someone is stealing his bottle of booze.

Bear Hollow near Ingham Station
Along Moonville Rail Trail
Along Moonville Rail Trail
39.308744, -82.304565

Bear Hollow and the Lost Hand

The tracks near Bear Hollow—an easy and little over a mile hike, (one way) from Moonville.

The last time anybody saw middle-aged coalminer Allan Albaugh was Saturday, August 24th, 1907. He had been drinking when he hopped on a train at Zaleski with a jug of whiskey in his hand and heading for his home in Luhrig near Athens. For several days, nobody heard from him, so a search party was sent out to find him. Soon enough, they discovered his hand near Moonville Tunnel.

While walking the tracks at Bear Hollow near Ingham Station, Frank McWhorter smelled something dead and found the rest of Albaugh rotted and covered in maggots. Later, some who walked the railroad from Moonville to Ingham Station said they saw a one-handed man walking the tracks with eyes peeled to the ground. It was Albaugh's ghost searching for his hand.

Warren County

Waynesville—
Museum at the Friends Home
115 S. 4th Street
Waynesville, Ohio 45068
39.531254,-84.090153

Ghostly Giggles

In the early 1800s, many Quaker families settled in and around Waynesville, leaving the south in protest of slavery. Among them was the Lynch family, who began erecting a home on the outskirts of town. Before the family's house was finished, the parents fell ill, and they sent their children to live with other families while mending. The father died. However, the mother, Jerry, lived and began searching for her children. She found all but one, a child named Mary.

Over the years, the town grew and the Friends Boarding Home for retired Quakers was built across from the site where the Lynch's home would stand. The boarding house was used for many years, and nowadays, the town is one of Ohio's most sought-after hotspots for antique shopping, and the Friends Boarding home is a museum. Caretakers sometimes hear the sound of a rocking chair moving, witness a figure on the front porch, and listen to ghostly giggles of a young girl they presume might be Mary. And some also believe her mother returns, still searching for her little daughter.

Waynesville—
Hammel House Inn and
Restaurant in Waynesville
121 S Main Street
Waynesville, Ohio 45068
39.529541,-84.087426

Ghostly Shenanigans of a Peddler

The Hammel House where a ghost resides—

In the winter of 1881, a photographer setting up a studio at the Hammel House tried in vain to take pictures for a customer. Each time he used his equipment, an old man dressed in early 1800s clothing would show up in the photograph behind the customers. If that was not enough, his photographic chemicals were upset, his lamp blown out, and his negatives ruined. Finally, the photographer was shaken so badly that he refused to stay at the inn any longer.

Old-timers knew the reason for the ghostly shenanigans, as the photographer's gallery was directly above an old well. In the 1820s, a peddler stopped to stay at the Hammel House and stayed in Room 4. When he did not show up in the morning, the owner sent a servant to awaken him. Although the man's clothing and suitcases were in the room and his carriage was left outside, his money was missing. Many believed that the inn's owner murdered the man and tossed him in an ancient well because he quickly sold the belongings and carriage of the peddler. After, visitors to the inn began witnessing a shadowy figure roaming from the room, down the stairway, and into the dining area, where it disappeared.

Peering into Room 4 at Hammel House where a ghost walks—

Waynesville—
Stetson House
234 S Main Street
Waynesville, Ohio 45068
39.528209,-84.087943

Dark-haired Woman

The ghost of a dark-haired woman in a high-collared dress roams the rooms of this building, cries softly, and peers out the windows. The 1810 house was originally the home of John Stetson's (Stetson's hats) sister—Louisa (Stetson) Larrick, who died there in 1879 of tuberculosis. Most believe the spirit is Louisa and at times, the ghostly smell of fresh gingerbread wafts through the house.

Waynesville—
Old Willie Anderson and
Mollie Hatte Property
Main Street
Waynesville, Ohio 45068
(private)

Murder on Main

A young girl's ghost appears along this street.

A ghost of a young girl named Myrtle will not lay to rest in Waynesville. Those taking the walkway down Main Street near her aunt's home she visited one late summer and the place she was murdered have seen the girl appear, then disappear—In late August of 1879, 37-year-old Mollie Hatte, her sister Clementine Weeks, and Clementine's 11-year-old daughter, Myrtle, were brutally murdered with a hatchet inside the small cottage Mollie resided with her 18-year-old son, Willie Anderson.

Main Street in Waynesville. Circa 1905. Courtesy Mary L. Cook Public Library

The home was on South Main Street in the quiet Quaker village of Waynesville. Although screams had been heard by neighbors the night of the murder, their decomposing corpses, one severely mangled by rats, were not discovered until nearly three days after when a rank odor began to seep out of the home. When neighbors showed concern that nobody had come and gone from the cottage for several days, a local constable and retired judge forced open the front door and were overwhelmed by the stench of death and the horrible sight of the three butchered bodies.

Authorities were never able to solve the ghastly triple murder—Willie, who was believed to have participated in or had guilt-ridden knowledge of the crime, committed suicide within a short amount of time and one particular motive never stood out among the others. Owners eventually demolished the home because of the unnerving sights and odd gurgling and hacking sounds. But the child occasionally still appears.

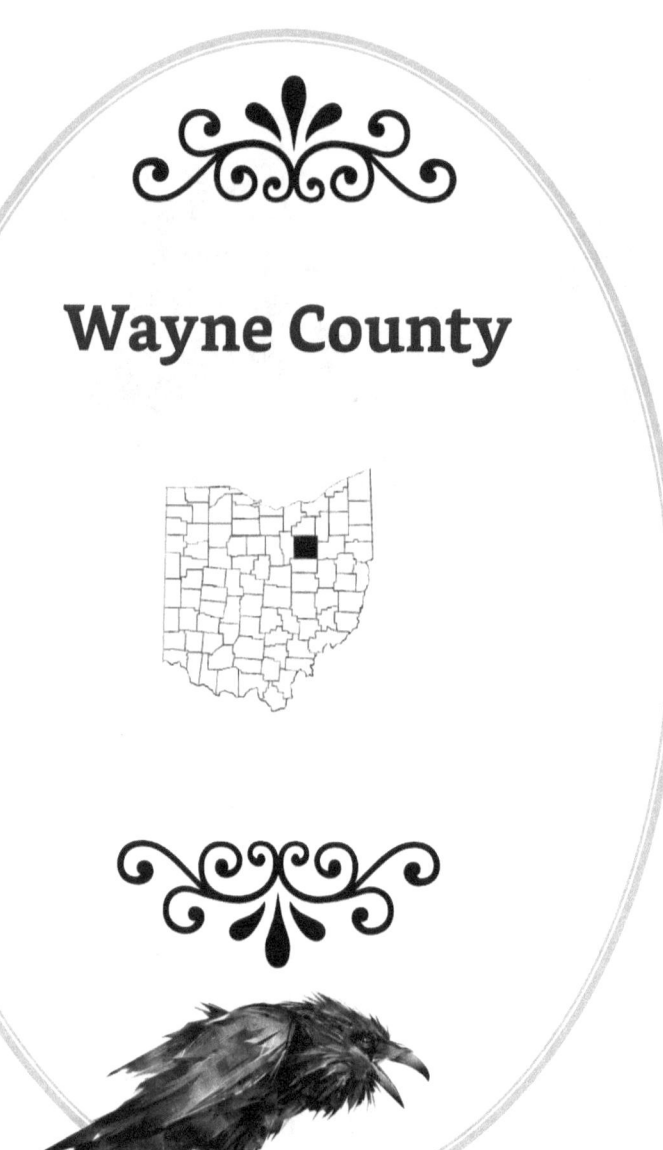

Wayne County

Chippewa Rogues Hollow Nature Preserve and Chidester Mill Museum
117514 Galehouse Road
Doylestown, Ohio 44230
40.941365,-81.67536

Rogues Hollow

The Mill Museum in Rogues Hollow—

It is a mysterious place, the little valley along Silver Creek a couple of miles from Doylestown. When men first began mining there in the 1840s, folks started calling it Peacock Hollow due to the streaks of rainbow colors in the split coal seams. Then a doctor from Akron came in, bought up the mineral rights, and dubbed the valley Rogues Hollow. Since the 1840s, over 50 mines sprang up in the area along with five saloons.

It was quite a wild town with a storied past of tough coal miners, nightly bar-room brawls, and lawlessness. Many rowdy miners traveled Rogues Hollow roads like Fraze and Clinton to work and home and back again. Once in a while, the ghostly grind of wagon wheels and the clop of mule hooves ride the night wind. The spectral blast of dynamite explodes from afar. Even shadowy figures appear on the old roads that miners used to walk.

The Chidester Mill — the road was built up the hill and away from the mill to avoid the rowdy mine town.

Nearby Chidester Mill was a woolen mill, sawmill, and dye house started by Samuel and Ephraim Chidester. It was in business from 1828 to 1888 and passed down through the family. During its earlier years, a young man making repairs on the mill fell into the machine, and the wheel crushed him to death. Many living in Rogues Hollow said they saw him return at dusk, strolling the paths of the mill long after he was dead to complete his work. In 1922, the owners replaced the original building with the structure used as a museum today, and his ghost still strolls around.

A young woman was spurned by her sweetheart when he discovered she was pregnant. When the child was born, she walked to the bridge over Silver Creek near the mill and tossed the baby into the cold waters. If you stand on the bridge, you can hear the child's wails. And you might even see the mournful mama. She stands along the edge, staring into the water, crying desperately to get her baby back.

The Crybaby Bridge where a young mother sacrificed her baby, and its anguished cries are heard.

An old tree grew on Clinton Road. It was called the Ghost Oak Tree because one night a tall horse galloping along the road collided with the tree and was killed. His ghost was seen under the tree for years, a dusky shadow beneath the limbs.

Bridge over Killbuck Creek
Overton Road
Burbank, Ohio 44214
40.925122,-82.007407

Leroy's Bridge

A man died after falling off the bridge over Killbuck Creek in the Overton Valley years ago. Soon after, passersby saw his ghost trudge up the bank and onto the road, where he faded away. Not long after, tiny lights danced in the woods around the bridge.

River Styx Trestle
256-262 E Ohio Avenue
Rittman, Ohio 44270
40.974941,-81.772252

Ghost Train Over River Styx

The trestle over River Styx in Rittman. Ghostly omen or just a ghost? You be the judge.

The Erie west-bound passenger train No. 5 was due in Mansfield at 8:56 a.m. on March 22, 1899. It was about a half-mile past Rittman and was heading toward Sterling at a rate of 60 miles per hour. Unfortunately, it did not make it on time. Sometime between 7:30 a.m. and 8:00 a.m., just as it crossed the trestle over a small stream named the River Styx (Styx River), the train jumped the track and rolled over.

All the cars, barring a dining car, derailed. Alexander Logan, the 48-year-old engineer, was crushed beneath the train.

Seven months later, a local Rittman doctor was returning home with a friend after visiting a patient. Just outside town, the two leisurely watched a train working its way down the tracks. It was almost to the short trestle running over the River Styx when the shrill whistle caused them to turn. Just as it got to the trestle, they heard the engine engage as if it was being placed in reverse before it burst into flames and smoke spilled into the air. The crash of metal and wood rang out along with the crackle of broken trestle timbers and the hissing of escaping steam. Shrieks from the pinioned victims echoed from the wreckage. Then the sights and sounds dissolved as if the horrific train crash did not happen at all.

Over the next year, more people reported seeing or hearing the ghost train following its doomed path across the River Styx train trestle. By April of 1901, when townspeople reported seeing a train wreck occur when no genuine train was nearby, it rattled more than a few who believed it had to be some forewarning of dire disaster. But no calamity ever came. The town is alive and well. The river still runs beneath the trestle, and trains run above. And perhaps, on moonless nights, the sound of the No. 5 sometimes makes its fateful run along the tracks, and the screams still pierce the air.

The River Styx
256-262 E Ohio Avenue
Rittman, Ohio 44270
40.974941,-81.772252

A Chippewa Legend of the River Styx

Railroad bridge where an old, old legend arose—

In the late evening on the night of October 21, 1827, two young men set out from the mouth of the River Styx in Rittman to where the railroad bridge now stands. They had heard a ghost lurked within the mists on that particular date and at the witching hour. It was dark, foggy, and the moon was nearly hidden by a cloudy sky as they paddled past the brush-filled shoreline to their destination.

The air was calm and dead; however, the night was alive with the call of owls and an occasional snarl or bark of a wolf. As the clock drew to midnight, light not much bigger than a lantern beam burst from the opposite side of the creek. Soon after, a bark canoe floated out and above the water with a beautiful Indian woman clothed in animal skins carefully adorned with pretty beads. Three times, she made a circle from one side of the creek to the other, then the woman and boat shot downstream, seeming to evaporate into the fog around it. A low and unsettling death song swept up from where the phantom had faded away. Abruptly, the canoe floated back into view, gliding toward the men with great force. The two shuddered, sitting erect, and prepared their paddles to flee. But just as they got their wits about them, the ghost disappeared and did not return.

They had seen the ghost! Before settlers farmed the land around Rittman, the Chippewa used the River Styx to travel through this region of Ohio. Around 1821, while several Indians were paddling along the river, they were attacked by a party of Delaware, Choctaw, and Mingo. During the battle, a young warrior who was soon to be betrothed was killed. When word came to the village that he had died, the young Chippewa bride-to-be was driven mad by the loss. She fled her home and disappeared into the woods around the River Styx. Years later, some would see the young woman's spirit at the creek at midnight on the 21st of each October.

Citations

Adams County Jail:
-Redden, Carla . "Ghost stories live on in Adams County ." The Ledger Impendent (Web log), October 31, 2012. Accessed http://www.maysville-online.com/news/ghost-stories-live-on-in-adams-county/article_92ea4e65-dafb-544a-a292-ccd4d3baa3fa.html.
-County Buildings at West Union. In E. N. W., & S. E. B., (Eds.). A history of Adams County, Ohio, 1900 (134-136). Milford, Ohio : Little Miami Pub. Co., 2000..
-Kelly, Stephen. "Legends and Landmarks of Old Adams" ,People's Defender, West Union, Ohio
-Image: The image is owned by the Stephen Kelley Memorial Scholarship fund which helps people who love, support and are still making history in the classroom and throughout the American Experience.
The Haunted Cave:
-The Haunted Cave. In E. N. W., & S. E. B., (Eds.). A history of Adams County, Ohio, 1900 (424-424). Milford, Ohio : Little Miami Pub. Co., 2000..
-Descendants of Herman Groethausen - Third Generation (Greathouse Point., 2008).
-Flatboat: Library of Congress Prints and Photograph LC-DIG-pga-01064
-Fletcher , M.(2011). (THE GREATHOUSE FAMILY OF OHIO COUNTY, (WEST) VIRGINIA AND BROWN COUNTY, OHIO.). November.
Mt Unger Cemetery:
-Henderson, Andrew, & (). Mount Unger Cemetery [Weblog post]. Retrieved April 1, 2014, from http://forgottenoh.com/Counties/Adams/mtunger.html
Serpent Mound:
- Ohio Historical Society. Serpent Mound: http://www.ohiohistory.org/museums-and-historic-sites/museum--historic-sites-by-name/serpent-mound/history [Brochure]. Ohio Historical Society.
Wickerham Inn:
- By Editorial Staff, State History Publications, LLC, Wickerham Inn. In L. K. Owen (Ed.), Ohio Historic Places Dictionary, Volume 2 (7-7). Somerset Publishers, Inc.
-Kelley, S.(). Legends and Landmarks of Old Adams . *People's Defender*, pp.
-Redden, C.(2012, October 31). Ghost stories live on in Adams County. The Ledger Independent , pp.
-Pioneers. In S. M. Kelley (Ed.), Adams County (pg 17). Charleston, SC : Arcadia, c2010..
Winchester Cemetery:
-McCann, B., Newman, B., & (). Winchester Cemetery- Winchester, OH (Ghosts) [Weblog post]. Retrieved from http://adamscountyghosthunters.weebly.com/
-History of Winchester Township [Weblog post]. Retrieved from http://www.rootsweb.ancestry.com/~ohcwinch/history.html
-The Highland weekly news. (Hillsborough [Hillsboro], Highland County, Ohio), July 23, 1863, Image 1
Ashtabula Train Disaster:
-Escher, S.(2009,). I-35 Bridge Collapse: Ashtabula River Railroad Disaster . Ashtabula River Railroad Disaster . Retrieved from http://35wbridge.pbworks.com/w/page/900664/Ashtabula%20River%20Railroad%20Disaster
-The Milan exchange., January 11, 1877, Image 2
-The Tiffin tribune., January 04, 1877, Image 3
-National Republican., Washington DC,December 30, 1876, Horror of Horrors
-Wilson, H.(1884, July 2). A Prize Venture. Abbeville Press and Banner, pp 1
Chestnut Grove Cemetery:
-Perrysburg Journal., Perrysburg, Wood Co. January 26, 1877West and South
-THE ASHTABULA DISASTER. Harper's Weekly—January 20, 1877
Images: Alexey Kuznetsov , Tiler84
Edgwood Cemetery and the McAdams Family:
-ancestry.com-The McAdams family of Ashtabula—census records
-Belamy, John Stark (Ed.). The The Last Days of Cleveland: and More True Tales of Crime and Disaster from Cleveland's Past. Gray & Company Publishers.
-Feather, Carl E, .. The McAdams mystery . Star Beacon
-Thomas, T.J. *Six White Stones*. The Wide World Magazine: An Illustrated Monthly of True Narrative, Adventure, Travel, Customs and Sport ..., 1913. Volume 30
-Ashtabula weekly telegraph., June 08, 1872.
-Howels, W. C. (1911, September 10). Did Ashtabula Have a Lucretia Borgia?. Cleveland Plain Dealer, pp. 53-53.
-Kingsville Public Library and Simak Welcome Center:
-Kingsville Public Library: www.kingsville.lib.oh.us
-Building historical info: Mariana Branch, Director-Kingsville Public Library

-images: Gale Wheeler
-Lakeview Paranormal-www.lakeviewparanormal.com/paranormal-investigation
-kingsville-public-library/
Louisa Catherine Fox:
-Coshocton Age September 24, 1869 -Almost A Suicide
-The Herald And Torch Light (Hagerstown, Md) February 17, 1869—A Terrible
Tragedy in Ohio
-New Philadelphia Ohio Democrat February 12, 1869—A Young Girl's Throat Cut
By Her Lover—The Murderer Attempts Suicide
-Hagerstown Mail Hagerstown Maryland February 5, 1869
-Greencastle Weekly Indiana Press March 30, 1870—The Scaffold
Salem Methodist Episcopal Cemetery:
-Centennial History of Belmont County, Ohio, and Representative Citizens, A. T.
McKelvey, Biographical Publishing Company, 1903 - Belmont County OH
Lady Bend Road:
-Charleroi Mail July 19, 1955, Turnpike Will Invade Premises of Ohio's Famed Lady
Bend Road
-Steubenville Herald Star July 28, 1924 Red Spoked Car Tourists Give Us a Call—
Pick Trail of Headless Lady.
Black Oak Road Ghost:
-www.forgottenoh.com/Haunts/**roads**.html
Old Egypt Cemetery:
http://www.graveaddiction.com/egypt.html
-www.midwestlost.com/locations/**ohio**/**belmont**/**egypt**search.html
Rankin House:
-Historic American Buildings Survey, E.F. Schrand, A. Hofmann, Photographers
November 20, 1936 WEST ELEVATION (SIDE). - Dr. John Rankin House, Liberty
Hill, Ripley, Brown County, OH
-http://www.ohioexploration.com/browncounty.htm
Clark:
-Springfield Prison: History of the Police Department of Springfield, Ohio: From the
Earliest Times in the Present with a Record of the Principal Crimes Committed,
Policeman's Mutual Benefit Assoc., 1909
-Natalie Fritz, Curatorial Assistant—Clark County Historical Society
Lucy Run:
-Historical Collections of Ohio ...: An Encyclopedia of the State: History Both
General and Local, Geography ... Sketches of Eminent and Interesting Characters,
Etc., with Notes of a Tour Over it in 1886, Volume 1, Henry Howe
H. Howe & Son, 1889
-Ancestry.com: Ezekiel Dimmit family tree, Charles Robinson family tree, Lucy
Dimmit, 1830, 1940, 1860 census.
-Springfield Globe Republic, November 29, 1885
-www.rootsweb.ancestry.com/~ohclecgs/cemeteries/lucyrun/index.html
-Hilda Lindner Knapp. Batavia Branch Reference Librarian, Clermont Cty, Oh
-www.findagrave.com/cgi-bin/fg.cgi?
page=gr&GSfn=lucy&GSiman=1&GScid=41885&GRid=21564866&
Dead Man's Curve:
-creepycincinnati.com/2011/11/11/clermont-county-dead-mans-curve/
Old Bethel Church and Cemetery
-www.rootsweb.ancestry.com/~ohclecgs/newsletter/bethalchu.html
-www.rootsweb.ancestry.com/~ohclecgs/cemeteries/oldbethel/index.html
Stepstone Landing:
-Spirit of Jefferson., January 30, 1866
Smyrna Cemetery
-www.rootsweb.ancestry.com/~ohclecgs/cemeteries/smyrna/index.html
Little Miami Bike Trail—Morgan's Raiders:
-www.clermont-county-history.org/.../morgans-raid-trail.html
-evansfamilytreeclimb.blogspot.com/2009_01_01_archive.html
-Gary Knepp, Civil War Historian— UC Clermont—Some *Clermont Countians
defiant during Morgan's Raid*- www.cincinnati.com/article/20130708/
EDIT02/307080090/Some-Clermont-Countians-defiant-during-Morgan-s-Raid
Ghosts of Roscoe Village:
-Grave Addiction: www.graveaddiction.com/roscoevil.html
-www.visitcoshocton.com/things-to-do/shopping/the-shops-of-roscoe-village-
Combs, Randy M., Swollen Itching Brain: Roscoe Village and Matilda Wade's Ghost -
coshoctonblog.blogspot.com/2006/06/roscoe-village-and-matilda-wades-
ghost.html
-The Coshocton Tribune (Coshocton, Ohio)-August 17, 1976, Tuck McConnell
Began Oldest Firm

Murder Ridge; Cletus Reese:
-Fear More Bodies Will Be Found on Farm of Former Mental Patient COSHOCTON. (1954, June 12). Logansport Pharos-Tribune, pp. 14
-Hunt More Bodies On Murder Ridge. (1954, June 12). Mansfield News Journal.
-Doubleyou. Now and Then (June 1956) Coshocton Tribune.
-Demented Killer's Half-Sister Sued. Lima News: (1956, June 6), pg. 12.
-Third Body Found on Reese Farm. (1954, June 11)The Coshocton Tribune: p1
-Henderson, [Weblog post]. Retrieved April 19, 2014, from www.forgottenoh.com/MurderRidge/murderridge.html

Mary Stockum:
-Ancestry.com—Stockum
-www.sleepyhollowpumpkins.com/legend_marystockum.htm
-www.graveaddiction.com/stockum.html
-1870 US Census—Linton Twp, Coshocton County
-Profile by Joanna Ross. (1967, Nov 11) Coshocton Tribune
-Map: Linton Township, Bacon P.O., Maysville, Plainfield P.O., Jacobsport
Atlas: Coshocton County 1872

Dead Man's Hollow:
-Murder. Huron Reflector (October 25, 1836)
-History of Crawford County, Ohio and representative citizens, John E. Hopley,Published 1912 by Richmond-Arnold Pub. Co. in Chicago, Ill . (pg 547 - 548) Dead Man's Hollow
-trees.ancestry.com/tree/6974196/person/6588515917/storyx/1a874ff2-e601-4a8e-95b5-87d93ba89343?src=search

Defiance County:
Henderson, A. [Weblog post]. Retrieved April 19, 2014, from www.forgottenoh.com/

Cole Stratford Cemetery:
-History of Delaware County and Ohio. O. L. Baskin & Co, 1880 (pg 312)
-Stratford Cemetery inscriptions: www.ohiogenealogyexpress.com/delaware/delco_cem_stratford.htm
-www.findagrave.com/cgi-bin/fg.cgi?page=cr&CRid=1982158&CScn=stratford&CScntry=4&CSst=37&CScnty=2060
-www.graveaddiction.com/colestrat.html

Fairfield County:
-files.usgwarchives.net/oh/fairfield/cemeteries/elmwoodc85cm.txt
-1883 History of Fairfield and Perry Counties, Ohio. www.perrycountyohio.us/fphhistory/
-LC-USZ62-74359, Library of Congress

Stillhouse Hollow:
-http://search.ancestry.com/cgi-bin/sse.dll?db=1860usfedcenancestry&indiv=try&h=43778863
- Hyde, Jesse. The geological history of Fairfield County (Ohio). Richmond-Arnold Pub. Co., 1912 Original from   University of Chicago Digitized8/17/11.
-Map and Markings: Jeff Camechis, Fairfield County Engineer's Office Administrative Assistant
-Christian Foglesong- The Lancaster gazette., September 25, 1851, Image 2
-Winnipeg Free Press March 19, 1881 Another Ghost Story
-The Vancouver independent., April 21, 1881, Image 3 A Ghost Story
-Map of Pleasant Township - Fairfield County, 1875
-Map of Fairfield County, 1849
-Barnes, Dwight. Lancaster Eagle Gazette, Friday February 22, 2002.*Tales from the past. Stories of mysterious murders, vagabonds and ghosts.*

Headless Horseman of Cherry Hill:
-The Fayette County Historical Society.
-Headless Horseman of Cherry Hill. In K. M. S. (Ed.), Buckeye legends (124-130). Ann Arbor : University of Michigan Press, c1994.
-Selected Histories of Fayette County Churches. Project requested by: Christopher Siscoe. Records compiled and printed by: Maria Wilburn.
-Haunted Hill. Gifts from Gail; notesfromgail.blogspot.com/2010_http://notesfromgail.blogspot.com/search?updated-min=2014-01-01T00:00:00-05:00&updated-max=2015-01-01T00:00:00-05:00&max-results=50
-Nearby Farmer has a Natural Gas Well, 1/11/57. Echo of Ghost Hill. Pg. 143

Washington Courthouse Cemetery:
-www.ohioexploration.com/fayettecounty.htm

Goll Woods and Cemetery:
--1850 United States Census
-New York, Passenger and Immigration Lists, 1820-1850

-Moulton, Geri. Williams County Genealogical Society-The Golls of Williams and Fulton County, Ohio. www.wcgs-ogs.com/peter_goll.htm

Clifton Gorge/John Bryan Park:
-Motes, LaVersa. Antiques Accent Old Spring Valley Home. Daily Gazette April 5, 1972. Xenia. Leap of Darnell
-Clifton History. Haunted Clifton. http://www.cliftonohiohistory.org/haunted_clifton.htm. http://www.johnbryan.org/clifton-gorge.html

Headless Horseman of Londonderry:
-http://bettyshinn.com/londonderry.aspx
-Wolfe, William G. Stories of Guernsey County, Ohio: History of an Average Ohio County. CHAPTER XXVIII Londonderry Township (864-883) 1943. Unigraphic in Evansville, Ind.
-US Atlas: Londonderry, Smyrna. Atlas: Guernsey County 1870. State: Ohio

Deep Cut:
-In O.Tom (Ed.), Haunted Highways (,218-218). Globe Pequot.
-Henderson, Andrew, & (). Deep Cut Ghost [Weblog post]. Retrieved April 7, 2014, from http://forgottenoh.com/Counties/Guernsey/deepcut.html

Old Washington:
-Map: Wills Township, Campells Station, Washington, Easton, Elizabethtown, Gombor P.O. Atlas: Guernsey County 1870
-Old Washington Presbyterian Church. www.owpresbychurch.com/history.html

Quaker City:
-Henderson, Andrew, & (). Mount Unger Cemetery [Weblog post]. Retrieved April 1, 2014, http://www.forgottenoh.com/Counties/Guernsey/513bridge.html
-Sarchet, Cryus B. History of Guernsey County Ohio. 1911. B.F. Bowen and Co. Indianapolis, Indiana.

Cincinnati Music Hall:
-Map: Cincinnati 1855 Mendenhall, State: Ohio. Publisher: Mendenhall
-Map: Cincinnati 1841 State: Ohio Publisher: Doolittle and Munson
-Quigley, C.Skulls and Skeletons: Human Bone Collections & Accumulations
- www.spmhcincinnati.org/Music-Hall-History/Haunted-Music-Hall.php
-"Biology Class Digs Deep for Bones". Dayton Daily News. June 16, 1994. Retrieved 2014-05-04.
-*Gossip About City Ghosts*. Cincinnati Commercial.
-Hearn, Lafcadio (October 22, 1876). "Gossip About City Ghosts". Cincinnati Commercial. p. 8.(courtesy: Information and Reference Department -Public Library of Cincinnati and Hamilton County
-Cincinnati City: Commercial Hospital. cincinnativiews.net/hospitals_part_2.htm

Cincinnati Union Terminal and Museum:
-Cincinnati Union Terminal. Cincinnati Museum Center. ww.cincymuseum.org/
-Flanders, Julia. U is for Union Terminal. julieflanders.blogspot.com/2012/04/u-is-for-union-terminal.html

Precht Bridge:
-Sandusky Star Journal November 30, 193. Ohio Briefs. Napoleon.

Ghost of Simcoe Valley:
-*The Ohio Democrat., November 29, 1900, Image 1—The Ghost of Simcoe Valley -- A Thanksgiving Story Founded on Facts and Misteries in Starr Township by A.L.O.*

Thomas McMahon Murder
-"FARMER FOUND DEAD: MONEY HOARD IS GONE" Democratic Banner 9/27/28
-From Newspaper Files Wednesday, September 28, 1938 Coshocton Tribune
-Seek Slayer of McMahon Coshocton Tribune March 1, 1931
-Gambier Man Held To Jury Newark Advocate May 16, 1929
-Ghost Stories Are Reviving Murder Probe The Newark Advocate May 1, 1929

Marion Lights:
-West, Dan. Marion County Ohio Railroad.www.west2k.com/ohstations/marion.shtml

Marion County:
-Jacoby, John Wilbur. The History of Marion County Ohio. The definitive history of Marion County and many of its citizens 1907 - Marion County (Ohio) - page 99
-The Marion Daily Mirror., March 31, 1909, Page 8
-Simpkins, J., & Hunt, S.. The Grave Marker with the Glowing Eyes . Retrieved May 22, 2014, from http://www.spookymarion.com/?cat=10&paged=3
-Kirby, D. Smith, K. Wilkins, M. Roadside Grave Of A Man Killed By A Tree, Marion, Ohiowww.roadsideamerica.com/story/10847

Spencerville:
-Gilbert, K. Haunted? United Methodist Church. Even Wesleys heard 'bumps in night'. umc.org/news-and-media/haunted-even-wesleys-heard-bumps-in-night.

Akron Civic Theatre:
-Mark, S., & McGuire, M. M. (Eds.). Weird U.S. (). Barnes & Noble Publishing.
Cuyahoga Valley National Park:
-Summit Metro Parks. www.summitmetroparks.org/parksandtrails/deeplockquarry.aspx
-The Belmont Chronicle. St. Clairsville, Ohio. October 16, 1890.Happenings of the week—Two Killed in Derrick Fall at Quarry.
-archiver.rootsweb.ancestry.com/th/read/OHSUMMIT/2001-04/0986914700
-Arizona"s New Immigration Law; The Tale of Two Soldiers-uselesstriviaandmindlessrants.blogspot.com/2010/04/arizonas-new-immigration-law-tale-of.html
-Brecksville—Summit County Map: 1874/-Summit County Map: 1891
Tuscarawas—Mary Seneff Ghost
-York Township, Mechanicsburg—Atlas: Tuscarawas County 1875
-The Stark County Democrat., March 03, 1881, Image
-Cleveland Plain Dealer. Ohio News 1881-03-16
-The Eaton Democrat., Mary Seneffs Ghost. April 07, 1881
-The Eaton Democrat. Ohio State News. April 14, 1881
-Memphis daily appeal. The Ghost of Murdered Woman Visits the Glimpses of the Moon. March 18, 1881.
-The Stark County Democrat. Missus Ellen A. Athey. March 03, 1881
-The Ohio Democrat. Murder Most Foul. New Phila Ohio, June 17, 1880
-The Ohio Democrat. The Murder of Mary Seneff. July 8, 1880
-The Ohio Democrat. The Murder of Miss Mary Seneff. June 24, 1880.
-Canal Dover, Tuscarawas County, Ohio 1899. Drawn by A. E. Downs. Published by T. M. Fowler & A. E. Downs." Library of Congress, Geography and Map Division
-Warlock's Grave:
-http://www.graveaddiction.com/rehobeth.html
-http://flashesinthedark.com/2009/05/17/ransoms-revenge-by-jamie-blair
-Warner, Beers, 1884 - Tuscarawas County (Ohio)
-Goshen Township- Atlas: Tuscarawas County 1875 L. H. Everts & Co. 1875
-http://trees.ancestry.com/tree/27836608/person/26014812725/mediax/4?pgnum=1&pg=0&pgpl=pid|pgNum
Winding Staircase:
-www.graveaddiction.com/win**stair**.html
-www.**ohio**exploration.com/**tuscarawascounty**.htm
Quarry:
-DeFeo,Susan. Haunted Houses Near New Philadelphia, Ohi. USA Today Travel Tips. http://traveltips.usatoday.com/haunted-houses-near-new-philadelphia-ohio-102825.html
-www.mix941.com/common/more.php?m=49&post_id=3891
Zoar and Vicinity:
-www.dispatch.com/content/stories/travel/2012/10/07/1-ghost-muster.html)
-Dark Shadow Ghost Tour. www.darkshadowghosttours.com/zoar-village.html
-www.ohioexploration.com/tuscarawascounty.htm
Rogues Hollow:
-CHIPPEWA ROGUES HOLLOW NATURE PRESERVE
and HISTORICAL PARK. 17500 Galehouse Road, Doylestown OH. www.chippewarogueshollow.org/
-Locher, Paul. Coal mining brings prosperity to Doylestown area. Daily Record.
-Frey, Russell. "Rogues' Hollow, History and Legends".
-Chippewa Township, Doylestown, Centerburg, Fox Lake Jct., Marshallville, Easton, Hametown Atlas: Wayne County 192x W. W. Hixson and co.
River Styx Bridge Train Wreck:
-ENGINEER KILLED And Fireman Fatally Injured by a Wreck on the Erie. Mansfield News, Mansfield, OH 22 Mar 1899
-Rittman, OH Train Wreck, Mar 1899. NEEDS LAUNDERING. Badly Damaged Mail Brought in From the Wreck at Rittman. Mansfield News, Mansfield, OH 23 Mar 1899
-Milton Township Atlas: Wayne County 1897

www.ingramcontent.com/pod-product-compliance
Lightning Source LLC
Chambersburg PA
CBHW051255250626
47155CB00009B/3301